I0653400

Always Her Cowboys

Cowboys Online : Moose Ranch, Volume 5

Jan Springer

Published by Spunky Girl Publishing, 2020.

Always Her Cowboys
Published by Spunky Girl Publishing
Copyright 2017 by Jan Springer
Discover other titles by Jan Springer at http://www.janspringer.com
Cover Art by Talina Perkins, Bookin It Designs

License Notes
This book is permitted for your personal use only.

Author Note

Always Her Cowboys

Cowboys Online 5

Moose Ranch

Jan Springer

JENNIFER JANE (JJ) Watson has spent ten Christmases in a maximum-security prison. The last thing she expects is to get early parole, along with a job on a remote Canadian cattle ranch serving Christmas holiday dinners to three of the sexiest cowboys she's ever met!

Rafe, Brady and Dan thought they were getting male ex-cons to help out around their secluded ranch, but instead they get an attractive and very appealing female. In the snowbound wilds of Northern Ontario, female companionship is rare. It's a good thing the three men like to share...

Christmas is coming once again to Moose Ranch and with the due date of JJ's baby approaching fast, JJ is distracting herself from anxiety attacks by keeping herself ultra-busy preparing for the arrival of her baby and planning Moose Ranch's first annual Christmas party!

In having a wee baby on the way, there's a lot of stress for Brady, Rafe and Dan. Especially due to JJ's decision on having a wilderness mid-wife deliver the baby at the ranch house - with all of them present for the birth! But their concerns don't stop the men from showing JJ how much they love her...out of bed and in!

With wicked snowstorms, a grounded bush plane, a cheerful holiday party and a sweet little baby, the owners of Moose Ranch know this will be one sparkling Christmas season they won't soon forget...

Stories in the Cowboys Online Series:

Cowboys for Christmas ~ Book One – Moose Ranch #1 Cowboys Online #1 -Free

Cowboys in Her Pocket ~ Book Two – Moose Ranch #2 Cowboys Online #2

Loving Her Cowboys ~ Book Three – Moose Ranch #3 Cowboys Online #3

Cowboys In Her Heart ~ Book Four – Moose Ranch #4 Cowboys Online #4

Always Her Cowboys ~ Book Five – Moose Ranch #5 Cowboys Online #5

Her Forever Cowboys ~ Book Six – Snowy Creek Ranch #1 Cowboys Online #6

Claiming Her Cowboys ~ Book Seven – Moose Ranch #6 Cowboys Online #7

Rescued by Her Cowboys ~ Book Eight – Moose Ranch #7 Cowboys Online #8

Chapter One

"BRADY! STOP! I SEE the perfect Christmas tree!" JJ shouted from behind Brady as he gunned the snowmobile across the sun-splashed, snow-covered meadow. Without even giving him a chance to slow down, she pounded on his back with her fists in excitement.

Brady grinned and kept driving at a quick pace. He needed to be careful though, especially with JJ being in her condition, but he also knew she enjoyed going fast and this wide-open debris-free meadow was the perfect place to give her that adrenalin fix.

He'd seen the attractive blue spruce tree, but he just wanted to tease her a little. He'd already picked it out himself a few weeks ago in late autumn when he'd been out this way with the all-terrain vehicle checking on a herd in the next pasture. But he hadn't mentioned the tree to her. He had wanted to surprise her.

"Brady!" she screeched and gave his back another smack.

"What?" he called out.

"The perfect tree! It's back there!"

"I can't hear you!"

JJ cursed, and he laughed. She was so cute when she got mad, but he didn't want her to get too angry. She was nine months pregnant, and it was two weeks before Christmas. They'd been so busy on the ranch that they'd been putting off looking for the tree. But this morning JJ had been insistent that today was the day to get their perfect holiday tree because Moose Ranch's first annual Christmas party that she was throwing, was only a few days away.

Despite a swelled belly that made it awkward for her to get around in the snow, she'd been ready after lunch and eager to go. He just wished she would take it a little easier with the house chores, but she was as stubborn as ever wanting to do everything. He loved her passion for her work, and he loved her.

"Brady!" she screamed near his ear and then she laughed.

Suddenly she wrapped her arms around his waist and hugged him. He chuckled as he realized she must have guessed that he was just kidding and that he had seen the tree. He slowed the snowmobile, turned, and then followed the tracks he'd just laid out in the snow. A minute later, he stopped right beside the tree, shut off the machine, and then he turned in his seat.

His breath caught at how stunning JJ looked in the late afternoon sunshine. She'd already removed her black helmet and glittering white snow dust floated around her head like a halo. Her cheeks were rosy red from the cold, her brown eyes sparkled with happiness and tussles of brown curls framed her pretty face.

"You're teasing me," she gasped. But before he could answer, she was already reaching behind her to where he'd strapped the snowshoes onto the back of the machine. She had hers on within a minute. Then she reached for his snowshoes and held them out to him.

"I saw it and yes, I was playing with you," Brady admitted as he accepted them.

"You best save the playing for tonight," JJ said with a wink.

Heat whipped through him at the huskiness in her voice. He knew her meaning. Tonight, was *his* night with her and this time around it would be Dan and Rafe who would just have to listen to her moans as he'd done on their respective nights with her. He felt no jealousy toward his two partners, only love and sometimes friendly teasing that couldn't be helped, as the three of them shared JJ.

As Brady strapped on one snowshoe and then the other, he couldn't stop thinking about his good luck in having a woman like her in his life. She was sweet, easy-going, and very compassionate and he was really looked forward to snuggling up with her in bed and talking about their unborn baby.

He was relieved that with her due date being so close she'd been instructed not to fly the bush plane until after the birth of their baby. He was ultra-glad that he wouldn't have to worry about her soaring through the clouds and maybe crashing the plane. He knew she was an excellent pilot, but he just could not get that niggling fear out of his system that he would lose her someday because of her love of flying.

His fear for her safety had only grown since that time several weeks ago when she hadn't come home due to a plane engine malfunction. He still shivered and woke up in a cold sweat some nights at what could have happened. Things could have been so much worse had JJ not managed to get that plane down the way she had. She'd suffered some pulled muscles in her back upon the crash landing and despite both a doctor and the midwife saying JJ and the baby were all right, he still wondered if that crash had harmed the baby in some way.

He wasn't so happy with her sudden decision a few weeks ago, of wanting to have the baby right here on Moose Ranch. With her anxiety and panic issues, he'd been convinced she would have preferred to be close to the hospital over in Thunder Bay. They had even made plans to stay in a hotel for a couple of weeks before her due date. But JJ had been told about a bush pilot mid-wife who was new to the area and JJ had wanted Rafe and Dan also present at the birth, which would have been impossible with them all staying in the city and no one running the ranch.

Brady bit down on the sharp spear of fear that suddenly gripped him. God help him if anything happened to either JJ or their baby due to them being hundreds of miles from the nearest hospital.

"Come on! Let's get the tree cut!" JJ's gleeful shout ripped him back to reality. She waddled to the trailer behind the snowmobile and grabbed the handsaw.

She was wearing a cute powder blue colored maternity snowsuit that had shown up in the form of a large package one day via the bush mail. Blue, from North Country Air, had flown in the parcel addressed to JJ. The suit had been a present from his sister, Jenna.

The garments came in very handy because JJ wasn't the shopping for maternity clothes type of girl, and she'd been wearing an ill-fitting older ski jacket of Rafe's for her cross-country skiing trips through the forest or her walks down to the frozen lake to grab the plane and take it up for an early morning fly.

But she'd been forced to stop flying at the insistence of the mid-wife who'd informed them that there was a higher risk of blood clots when a pregnant woman was in the air close to her due date.

"Come on! What are you waiting for?" JJ called out and waved the handsaw at him, gesturing for him to follow.

He grinned. That pregnant woman moved quite fast through the fluffy white snow. He wished he could move just as quick, but he still had some lingering difficulties with walking due the tetanus infection he'd had several months earlier. The disease had damaged the nerves in his legs and other parts of his body. But he was confident the stiffness and pain would eventually go away. The doctors had said it took time for damaged nerve endings to heal. He just needed to stay patient.

Brady stepped onto the snow, removed his helmet, and placed it beside JJs on the seat. Then he followed her tracks. When he reached the towering tree, he had sudden doubts that it would fit into the ranch house. But with JJ's beaming smile, he didn't have the heart to break the news of his suspicion to her, so he quickly set to brushing away the snow from the trunk, accepted the saw from her and began to cut.

"It is the most beautiful tree I have ever seen. It has such a lovely bluish tinge to it. It's a shame to cut it down," she whispered from beside him.

He stopped cutting and gazed up at her. She was staring at the tree like some little kid who'd just seen something so wonderful that she couldn't believe it. But JJ was like that. She appreciated everything because she'd lost so many years in prison.

Suddenly the bright sunshine disappeared, and Brady surveyed the sky. Dark, ominous clouds had taken over the sun. The wind felt colder, and giant snowflakes began to gently swirl upon them.

Shit. The weather forecast had called for a snowstorm later today. It appeared it was already here. A bit of unease draped over him. He shouldn't have allowed JJ to talk him into this trip. They could have waited until after the storm. He should have radioed Rafe and Dan too and let them know they were heading out to get a tree. Instead, he'd just left a note on the dining room table.

If something happened here...Brady shook his head and brushed off his uneasiness. He had to hurry and get them back home. He returned his attention to the tree and cut fast. A couple of minutes later, the tall tree cracked and began to sway.

"Timber!" JJ called out.

Brady scrambled out of the way, slipped his arm around JJ's waist, and watched the tree fall into the white snow with a loud poof. Then everything went completely silent except for the faraway sound of a woodpecker cracking its beak on a tree.

"It's gorgeous, Brady. Absolutely, gorgeous!" JJ whispered as she tenderly touched one of the prickly-looking blue-green branch tips with her gloved hands.

He had to admit, they did have great taste in trees.

"Here, hold this saw and I'll grab the tree," he instructed.

A few moments later, the tree was tucked safely on the trailer and Brady sighed with relief when the snowmobile roared to life. With any luck, they'd be back to the ranch house within the hour.

Dan stared out the kitchen window at the swirling snowflakes and the increasing darkness. Worry screamed through him as he strained to see any sign of lights from an incoming snowmobile.

"They're still not back?" Rafe called as he stomped down the stairs. He'd taken a quick shower, and he was towel drying his hair as he strolled into the kitchen. They'd returned about half an hour ago to find a note on the kitchen table stating Brady and JJ had gone Christmas tree hunting. They'd left at one this afternoon and it was now four.

He had a bad feeling about this. JJ was always humming around in the kitchen at this time of afternoon cooking supper. And Brady should have known better to go out alone without them especially with a snowstorm coming and they had taken only one machine. If it broke down...

Dan shook off that uncomfortable idea and inhaled a deep shuddering breath.

"Nothing but white," he replied, trying to act cool. But his insides were twisting with sickness and worry.

Where the hell are you?

"Did you try to hail them again on the satellite phone?" Rafe asked. Dan picked up the urgency lacing Rafe's voice.

"Still no response," he admitted.

"They could be in a gorge or something and not picking up the signal. Okay, I'll load us with coffee and let's get back out there and follow their trail," Rafe said as he grabbed a couple of Thermos from a nearby shelf.

"No trail to follow. Snowing like a bitch out there."

"Seriously?" Rafe asked.

He stepped in beside Dan and let out a low whistle as he stared out the window.

"Everything is freaking white. Can't see a thing. We'd better get our asses in gear," Rafe said in a rush as he reached for the steaming coffee pot. "I'll put some food together too. You grab the emergency kit and pack some warm blankets and pocket warmers in a plastic bag and—"

Dan nodded, and he was already halfway across the kitchen when he realized Rafe had stopped speaking. Dan turned and noticed Rafe had returned to the window and was gazing out. He was frowning.

Dan's gut wrenched. Did Rafe think the storm was too serious for them to go out in? Suddenly an odd sound drifted through the quiet room. The low hum of an engine? At first, he couldn't be sure. Didn't want to get his hopes up. It could just be a low-flying bush plane passing over, but then the rumble grew louder and more distinct.

Relief poured through Dan. Rafe gave a whoop of joy that would have woken the dead. Dan's uneasiness forgotten; he raced Rafe down the hallway. He pushed open the door and they scrambled into the mudroom, grabbed their coats off the hooks and headed toward the back door where they saw the flash of lights shine through the frosted windows.

Thank God! They were back. They were home.

JJ was so glad to see the ranch house as Brady drove the snowmobile into the front yard that she almost burst out crying from happiness. She was cold, she was hungry and for the last little while she'd been fighting off a bad case of nerves as she wondered how in the world Brady could see where he was going in this storm.

As she lifted her helmet, icy snowflakes blasted her face. She couldn't see anything through all the whirling snow. It was a miracle Brady had been able to find their way back at all.

Suddenly there were shouts from the house and she gazed up to see Rafe and Dan struggling into their coats as they stomped down the ranch house stairs.

"Get your asses inside!" Dan's shout alerted her that he was pissed off.

Thankfully though, a moment later, Rafe's protective arm curled around her waist, taking away her momentary shock at Dan's gruff attitude. Before she could ask what was wrong with Dan, Rafe helped her off the snowmobile and placed her helmet back onto her head and Dan was sliding onto the seat that Brady had just vacated.

"Wait! Bring the tree inside!" JJ shouted into the shrieking wind the instant she realized Dan was going to start the snowmobile and take it and the trailer with the tree to the shed.

She heard Dan curse. Then she grinned when he shook his head and his shoulders slumped in defeat. It appeared all his anger had suddenly disintegrated. Good. Now the men could trim the tree while she prepared supper.

"Get inside, both of you, before you catch your death. Rafe and I will get the tree into the mudroom," Dan yelled. She nodded and suddenly understood why he was mad. He'd been worried about them.

Brady grabbed her chilled hand and tugged her up to the ranch house. A moment later, warm welcome air breathed against her as she and then Brady entered the safety of the mudroom.

"Nice to be back, eh, sweetheart?" Brady asked as he removed his helmet and then helped her off with hers. Then he unzipped her jacket.

"For a little while I thought we'd never make it," she admitted as she tore off her gloves. The suit that his sister had sent was a godsend. It had kept her and the baby quite warm against the frosty snowstorm. But she had started to feel a bit chilled about half an hour ago when the wind had picked up.

"Tell you the truth, I was starting to get a bit nervous myself," Brady chuckled as he slid off his gloves.

"But we made it home safe and sound and with the tree, that's all that matters. Right?" JJ asked.

Now that she was thawing out and had a chance to collect her thoughts, she understood why Dan and Rafe were upset. Was Brady just as upset with her?

He didn't answer as he helped her off with her coat.

Oh dear.

"I'm sorry I talked you into taking me out today. I should have listened to you—"

He reached up and placed a finger on her mouth.

"Shh, you didn't do anything wrong. I heard the weather forecast too. I thought we had time. I'm the one who made a mistake. Not you," he said softly.

"But—"

"No, don't go there, JJ. We made it back. Everything turned out just fine. We got our tree, and we know the risks living out here."

She nodded, and he slid his finger off her mouth.

"You are so good to me, Brady."

"I'm just glad you and the baby are safe. Nothing else matters."

She could tell by his words and by his serious expression that he was feeling guilty for caving into her urgency of going out today. It was best to drop this subject and let this end right here and now. No use in dwelling on it. It would just send her into a panic attack and ruin the evening she had planned.

"And nothing else matters that you are safe too," she added.

Good heavens, because of her stupidity, Brady could have been hurt.

"Stop, JJ. Stop thinking about it," Brady warned gently.

Despite the seriousness of what might have happened, JJ couldn't help but laugh at how Brady seemed to be able to read her mind.

"Okay, you caught me! I'm stopping!" She threw her hands up in the air.

She'd have to whip up something special for the guys tonight. Maybe some beer brownies as an apology for her impulsiveness where the tree was concerned. But when she'd heard on the radio that a huge storm was going to hit later in the day, she'd panicked and twisted Brady's arm in taking her out before the storm arrived.

"I'll get supper warmed up. And don't think that I've forgotten tonight is our night," she said after she slid off her boots and struggled out of her suit pants.

The sweet grin that touched Brady's lips made her heart thump with lightning speed.

"I'm looking forward to it, sweetness," he replied.

She had a feeling that he might kiss her, but Rafe shouted at them to open the door because the tree was coming in.

"Get into the house before you catch cold," Brady warned.

JJ nodded and hurried out of the mudroom before she caught the blast of cold air as Brady rushed to let the guys in with the tree.

Oh! Tonight was going to be so much fun getting that tree trimmed and decorated. She could hardly wait!

Chapter Two

"JJ, YOU SURE KNOW HOW to pick a beautiful Christmas tree," Rafe said with a chuckle from beside JJ as all four of them stood in front of the giant, plump tree.

"She sure does," Brady replied softly as he slid an arm around her waist and gave her an affectionate squeeze.

"I swear this is the most beautiful tree I have ever seen," JJ gushed as she admired the sparkling ornaments and Christmas lights.

Dan laughed. "You say that every year."

"And I mean it every year," JJ said as happiness burst through her. "I love this time of the year. The snow sparkles beneath the sunshine and the property looks like a magical winter wonderland with Christmas trees everywhere."

The guys all smiled and nodded.

This tree certainly was different than the ones she'd had when she'd been a kid. Back then it had just been her mom and herself. Despite her mother working two minimum wage jobs, they'd been poor. But her mom made sure they had a tree every year, even if it was a scraggly one. Often, she would get the last tree at the local tree lot, and it was usually free in the last couple of hours before the lot people closed down for the season on Christmas Eve. But those trees, just like this one, had been real and smelled nice, not fake-scented like the plastic ones she hadn't been able to stand looking at while she'd been in prison.

If she stared hard enough at this tree, she could almost see her mother standing there, a tender smile on her face as she nodded her approval at picking such a lovely tree.

"Merry Christmas, sweet pea," she'd whisper and hug her warmly. Those earlier years of her life had been happy ones, and she always missed her mom, mostly though, around this time of the year.

But thoughts of her not being alive couldn't bring JJ down this evening. There was an unusual giddiness embracing her tonight. Maybe it had to do with the narrow escape from the nasty storm and how lucky they'd been for Brady to find his way back in the whiteout conditions. Or more than likely because after dinner they'd popped popcorn and strung it into long chains and placed them beside the Christmas lights on the tree branches.

That had been followed with them hanging the fragile glass ornaments; angels, frosted pinecones, and round ornaments with fancy designs that Brady's sister, Jenna, had sent JJ's first Christmas here.

They'd hung all the ornaments and some silver tinsel and this year she'd added store-bought candy canes, some cute pinecones she'd gathered this fall during her walks in the nearby forest, and she'd tied some puffy red and black plaid ribbons that she'd created herself with some fabric from an old tattered shirt of Dan's to the tips of some of the branches.

Before putting up the tree though, it had had to lose about three feet from the base in order not to hit the ceiling, but that had been taken care of before supper by Dan out in the mudroom.

Now it was almost eleven o'clock. Outside, the wind howled, and icy blasts of snow pummeled the glass panes of the frosted windows, but it was toasty and delightful in here in the living room. The guys had taken turns stoking the fire in the nearby hearth and while they all had decorated the tree, they'd sung Christmas carols.

"I know it's a bit late, but how about that dessert I promised. I have beer brownies hidden in a cupboard," she said after she noticed the guys had grown quiet.

Reluctantly, she turned away from the beauty of the tree but stopped short when Brady refused to loosen his grip around her waist.

"You're all the dessert we need tonight, Jennifer Jane," Brady whispered.

Oh, how sweet.

"I've decided because of what happened today, that I'm making an exception to our one-on-one time together. Tonight, it will be all of us together. It will help everyone heal. But only if you agree."

Her breath caught at Brady's lusty gaze and then she observed Rafe and then Dan. Their eyes sparkled with sexual arousal.

Excitement snapped through her. Although she'd gained plenty of weight due to her growing baby, and her tummy was near to busting and her back ached most of the time now, she enjoyed these intimate moments with her cowboys. Loved that they still wanted her even when she looked like a giant whale.

"What do you gentlemen have in mind?" she purred. Heat poured through her as Brady let go of her waist and all three men surrounded her.

Rafe reached for the hem of her maternity top.

"We're anything but gentlemen, tonight," Rafe whispered.

"So, you're going to ravage me, are you?" she teased.

"Over and over," he replied in a hoarse voice.

Earlier, when it had grown hot in the living room because of the crackling fire, she'd gone upstairs to change out of her pants, long johns, heavy sweater, and layered tops, and then slipped into a white pair of maturity pants and a cute red maternity top with the *words I've been a Naughty Girl* scrawled across the baby bump area.

As Rafe's hot knuckles brushed against her bulging tummy, he smiled.

"We've decided we're going to make those words on your top come true," he said thickly.

JJ giggled. She liked the sound of that.

His gaze held hers as she raised her arms and Rafe lifted off her top. He tossed it onto the nearby couch.

Over the past few weeks, her breasts had grown so heavy that she'd been forced to purchase a maternity bra on her last trip to the city and now Brady and Dan didn't waste any time in helping her out of the garment. Her breasts spilled free and warm air splashed against her large sensitive nipples.

Dan let out a slow whistle.

"Beautiful, baby. Absolutely beautiful," he whispered as he studied her bared breasts.

Her pussy clenched, and her thighs trembled as Dan licked his lips and both he and Rafe moved closer. With her every breath, she inhaled their scents. They smelled of spruce and of passion.

"We're going to eat you up, sweetness," Rafe muttered. His voice was husky, his brown eyes dark with sensuality.

She gasped as their calloused hot hands cupped her breasts and both men's heads lowered. She keened and jerked as their hot lips ensnared her nipples. Their tongues lapped, and their mouths sucked until sensations cascaded over her and she was drowning in pleasure.

"Kick off your slippers and spread your legs, baby," Brady muttered from behind her. The tone of his lust-thickened voice was like an aphrodisiac, turning her mindless and obedient.

She did as he instructed, and trembled when he dipped his hands beneath the elastic waistband of her pants and panties. His fingers were hot as they scorched her flesh. He pulled her garments over her ass and hips and then lower. With Rafe and Dan both suckling her nipples, she was able to slap her hands upon their strong, muscular backs for support and managed to step out of the clothing.

Then the heated length of Brady's body pressed against her back and her backside. The unmistakable knot of his erection ground against her bottom making her crave for sex the old-fashioned way, but because of the baby, she knew the three men wouldn't make love to her by penetration. They had other naughty ways...

Brady lifted her hair and kissed the nape of her neck with feather-like touches and his warm hands smoothed over her sides, her hips and then her thighs, stoking the fires igniting inside of her. He sucked her left earlobe into his hot mouth, making her moan. His sensual lips sipped her flesh and the pleasure he created made her tremble and ache for more.

She let her head drop back against Brady as he continued kissing her body. His mouth made love to the length of her neck, his lips touching her sensitive flesh with feather-like brushes. He splashed kisses across her shoulders and then along her upper back, making a delicious storm of desire rage within her.

Rafe and Dan tugged at her nipples, their succulent mouths licking and teasing the tight peaks until she writhed and wiggled beneath the pleasure.

"Brace yourself, sweetheart," Brady suddenly warned as he gently pushed her away from him and closer to Dan and Rafe.

Brady's calloused hands sailed seductively along her sides and then settled over her full hips, and she knew he'd dropped to his knees. She whimpered as she realized he was going down on her.

Instinctively, she spread her legs and tensed with anticipation.

A moment later, Brady's warm breath blew against her pussy lips, and she moaned as a finger slipped between her labia and dipped into her throbbing vagina.

"You're creaming up a storm, babe," Brady whispered from below.

His breathing was ragged, and she couldn't think as he withdrew his finger and then sucked her throbbing labia into his mouth. She gasped as his teeth softly latched onto her flesh and then he tugged her pussy lips until she burned. The intimate pulling made her cry out in frustration. She wanted more. Needed more from him. She struggled to form her thoughts, to put them into words, but no sentences escaped her mouth.

"Brady," she managed to puff.

Her breaths quickened as Dan and Rafe sweetly massaged her weighty breasts, their fingers kneading her flesh, their eager mouths sucking her nipples, hard and furious. She bucked and keened as sensations gathered through her.

Her inner thighs quaked and trembled and she could do nothing but moan her joy as Brady let go of her labia and then slurped his hot tongue, strong and demanding, over her sensitive clit.

Over and over. He licked and lapped, and sucked her throbbing flesh until she was a shivering mess and crying out from the waves of tremors rocking into her.

Brady stroked and pulled and then lapped and licked some more. He made love to her pussy and Dan and Rafe made love to her breasts and nipples until the coiled need and pleasure buried deep within her burst.

She lost her senses and soared out of her self-control. Her thoughts spiraled as wicked sensations, tight and sharp, snapped through her.

She bucked and gyrated, gasping at the sultry vibrations that sizzled through her as if she were being electrified. Exquisite pleasure pummeled her. Ecstasy gripped her, and she spiraled inside of sparkling stars and rode the colorful bows of rainbows. She danced within the land of joy and unconditional love, the killing pleasure pouring through her with demon-like speed, sucking her into a pulsating center of a wild uncontrollable frenzy of which there was no escape.

THE NEXT FEW DAYS FLEW by quickly. Before JJ knew it, the Christmas party she had planned was only an hour away and she was a nervous wreck. What *had* she been thinking of arranging a party so close to her due date? Her back was aching, her breasts felt incredibly heavy, and she waddled instead of walked as she made a last inspection of the bedrooms.

Blue, Kaley, and Kelly had been kind enough to offer to pick up Mitch, Daegen, and Paul over at their ranch, via Blue's bush plane. Blue had outfitted her plane with skis for the winter, to continue her mail route into the most desolate areas of Northern Ontario where some people preferred to live.

All JJ's guests had said they would be leaving tonight after the party, but JJ had insisted the guys set up the cots and get the rooms ready just in case everyone decided to stay. Better to be safe than sorry, was her motto.

As she entered Dan's bedroom, she gazed out the nearest window and surveyed the ranch surroundings. She smiled as warmth and happiness bubbled through her. Although it was already dark outside, everything looked so Christmassy. White plumps of snow drenched the trees and the ground, and long icicles hung from the eaves of the barn, the outbuildings, and the wood-rail fencing around the corrals and bright red and green lights sparkled in the snow-covered boughs of the scraggly pine trees that straddled the cleared path leading down to the lake. From here she could even see the cute snowman that Brady had created a couple of days ago. To greet their guests, he'd said. She loved that about Brady. Every once in awhile, he let his inner kid shine through, and she knew instinctively he would be the best father.

It had snowed off and on almost every day and night since the beginning of November and it was doing so now too. From here she could barely see the lake because of the darkness of late afternoon and the harried swirl of snowflakes that almost drowned out the silhouettes of the guys, who were busily clearing a runway on the frozen lake with the riding snow blowers. The men had also placed several gas lanterns on both sides of the runway so Blue could easily land her plane when she arrived.

JJ had even invited Layla, her midwife, to the party, but she had called earlier this morning to cancel because she was off to deliver an earlier than expected baby a couple of hundred miles away.

JJ tore her gaze away from the pretty scenery and returned to inspecting the room.

Thankfully, the guys had done a wonderful job putting clean sheets on all the spare beds and setting up some spare cots too or JJ would have been in trouble because she could barely bend due to stiffness in her back. The smell of turkey baking in the oven made her mouth water and as she maneuvered her way down the stairs, she gasped as the baby suddenly decided to give her a good punch to her belly.

Ow, that hurt. Despite the pain, JJ smiled and gazed down at her swollen tummy. A small fist was outlined against her top.

"Sweetie, you need to settle down. It's not your time yet," JJ whispered and gently patted the baby's tiny fist. The sweet lump disappeared, and JJ blew out a tense breath as she waited for the pain to decimate. It went away, and she wobbled the rest of the way down the stairs. The mouthwatering smell of turkey was stronger down here and she couldn't wait until all their guests were here.

Boy, but she was hungry! And in the way the baby was rolling around inside, she or he was hungry too.

In the kitchen, JJ slipped on the oven mitts, opened the oven door, and stood back as a blast of hot herb-scented air blew against her face. She recognized the rosemary, basil, oregano, and sage Dan had planted and then picked and dried this autumn from their garden. The smells complimented each other very nicely, making her mouth water.

She pulled out the grill with the giant roaster, lifted the lid and placed it upon her cutting board, grabbed the baster, and gave the turkey a generous final basting.

Wow! The giant bird looked immaculate. Its skin glowed a golden brown and juices flowed and bubbled. Her guests would enjoy this bird, for sure. When she finished the basting, JJ left the lid off and slid the turkey back into its place. A moment later, she gave the dinner table a final inspection.

The theme was simple and traditional with the coloring red, white and gold, along with homemade evergreen and pine swags laden with long stem red candles. She'd set a red tablecloth and because they didn't have any fancy dishes, she'd placed the plain white ones.

She'd given the place settings some pizzazz with fancy folded green napkins and written in gold pen each guest's name on a card, so he or she would know where to sit.

Another swift kick within caused JJ to gasp from the pain. Baby was getting rowdy again. A bit of nervousness skittled through her at the thought that maybe the baby was coming early? And with Layla away on another call...maybe it had been a bad idea to have her firstborn here on the ranch? What in the world had she been thinking? What if something went wrong? What if something bad happened to the baby? What if—

Reign it in, JJ. Reign it in. Layla said the baby might become more active closer to your due date and not to panic.

JJ inhaled slowly and then exhaled. Okay, she was not going into labor tonight. And even if she did go into labor, Rafe had delivered Blue's baby without much of a problem.

Despite trying to talk herself down before anxiety took a firm hold, that inner nervousness persisted as she waddled into the hallway and to the first-floor bedroom where she'd lain out her Christmas clothing.

JJ's heart fluttered at the pretty dress she'd ordered online. It was a raspberry-colored stretch jersey dress with a cute crossover V-neckline in front and back, allowing her to wear it off the shoulders or on. Tonight, she opted to wear it on the shoulders.

As she slipped on her flat black shoes, another recent purchase, due to her slightly swelling feet, she heard the guys stomping up the back stairs and enter the mudroom.

"Wow! Smells really good in here!" came Rafe's shout as he entered the hallway.

JJ brightened now that her men were home. Before clearing a runway for Blue, they'd been out with the snowmobiles and trailers loaded with hay for the cattle in the one of the closer sections of their property.

An all-day job for them would have taken her only a couple of hours with the plane, but because of her current condition, she was grounded.

"Wow! Beautiful!" Dan said as he stopped in the open doorway and peered into the bedroom where she'd just changed into the dress. He was joined by Brady and Rafe, who peeked in over Dan's shoulder.

Appreciation sparkled in their gazes and her three cowboys suddenly whistled in unison.

"Hot and sexy," Brady murmured. His voice was thick and hoarse. Full of lust and love.

"Sweet and sensual," Dan complimented with a wink.

"Any other night, baby..." Rafe let his words trail off and shook his head slowly.

JJ laughed. She knew what Rafe meant. Any other night and they'd be undressing her, loving her and they'd all be late to dinner.

But with their guests about to arrive, her men appeared to be well-behaved, or they would have quickly peeled her out of her dress.

Well Rafe wasn't behaving, for he suddenly dashed away. He shouted that he was getting the upstairs shower. Dan swore, and he and Brady raced for the bathroom across the hall. Dan won as the door slammed shut in front of Brady.

JJ tried hard not to laugh as Brady returned. He stopped a foot away from her and stared. He was shaking his head as if in wonder.

"Just stay there, baby. Just let me look at you. Let me remember you this way, because soon you'll just be a skinny lady again."

JJ gasped with mock shock and swatted his broad chest. "Just skinny! Are you saying I'm fat now?"

Brady laughed and grabbed her wrists before she could smack him again.

Oh, he looked so damned sexy with a scruffy five o'clock dark shadow hugging his chin and cheeks. His gaze darkened, and his head lowered. Her heart thumped with a maddening speed as he stopped mere inches from her mouth. She parted her lips, eager for his love.

"I want you so bad, Jennifer Jane, that it hurts," he whispered.

"Me too," she answered.

She ached so much for him to make love to her. For all her men to make love to her again. But they'd held off on sexual intercourse in order to protect the baby.

Cold air blew off him, but it did little to cool her down.

"You're cold from the outdoors," she said. Sympathy for his comfort rocked her. She should be letting him go, urging him to go up to her room and use her shower to warm up. But she just loved the way he looked at her. His blue eyes lit with sparkles of love and his hands held her so firmly, yet so gently.

"Not as cold as the other day when we got that Christmas tree. Remind me to properly punish you after the baby gets here. Punish you for being such a vixen that I cannot say no to you. In the meantime..."

His lips were hot and firm as they melted with firm possession over hers. He caressed her mouth, every stroke making the sensual tension mount within her. Before her anticipation could soar to a maddening pleasure, Brady broke the kiss. She whimpered her frustration.

He moved his head away, blew out a tense breath and closed his eyes. A muscle twitched in his left cheek, a sign of his self-control.

"Oh man, JJ, you're killing me here," Brady growled.

"You're killing *me*," she breathed harshly. Her legs trembled with excitement and when he let go of her wrists, she grabbed him by his sweater, and held him, preventing him from leaving. Then she splayed her hands over his warm chest, felt his muscles bulge beneath the wool.

"We're not done, Brady," she teased, allowing her wild side to unleash. She leaned closer and kissed him full on his succulent mouth. Pleasure rocked her, and a guttural growl ripped from his chest and into her mouth. His tongue followed the animalistic noise and he sensually stroked between her lips.

She jolted as he mated with her tongue, touching, swirling, and probing. He made her body hum. Made her feel loved. Made her want more.

A grumbling noise broke through JJ's pleasure. *Plane*, she thought numbly.

But his scorching kiss held her attention and she instinctively pressed herself harder against Brady. His body was solid and muscular, and he always made her feel so safe and able to be herself. He always ignited the flames of need and the naughty girl buried deep inside of her. Just as he was doing now.

She could feel his desire for her coiled inside of him and the restrained tension in his kiss. She was surprised when he curled his hands over her shoulders and lowered the sleeves. Due to the dress allowing her to nurse, when the time came, the garment was easy for him to maneuver, and her plump breasts easily spilled free. She hadn't worn a bra because the dress had one sewn right into it.

"Brady," she moaned as she watched him lick his lips. Suddenly she wanted his mouth on her flesh.

JJ inhaled as Brady cupped her breasts and then dipped his head. She moaned with pleasure as he drew an engorged nipple into his mouth. He sucked gently as he kneaded her other breast with his hand.

She moved her belly against his, gyrated her hips and tried hard to ignore the warning in her head that yes, she could hear an approaching plane outside. But Brady's mouth felt so wonderful as he sucked. Her pussy grew hot and wept with a fierce need for penetration.

She whimpered her distress and then suddenly Brady stopped.

Oh shoot. No.

He groaned and moved his head away from her breast.

"They're here," he mumbled. He ran a hand over his beard stubble and then frowned.

Who is here? She numbly thought and then like an ice-cold avalanche it suddenly hit her that guests were coming to dinner.

Her legs trembled, and she quickly blew out tense breaths and rearranged her clothing. Her face felt hot as he just stood there and watched, a needy look on his face, his lips red from suckling her nipple. She had no doubt he would masturbate in the shower now that he was aroused. Oh, how she wished she could join him.

"Go! Upstairs to my room and shower in there! I'll greet the guests," she urged. But before he could go, she reached out and grabbed him.

"Your clothes! They're all cleaned and pressed. Don't forget your clothes!" She shrieked as a sudden burst of panic shot through her.

He gave her a look as if to say, where are they?

Her men! If she didn't dress them, then they would show up to the party wearing their work clothes!

She nodded to the bed. She'd lain out a freshly laundered pair of pants and a shirt for him on the opposite side of the bed where she'd had her dress. She'd also put fresh clothing out on Rafe's bed and on Dan's bed.

Brady chuckled and went to the other side, bundled everything into his arms and then came around and headed toward the door.

JJ nodded her approval, her panic ebbing. She pushed past him.

Had they not stopped when they did, they would have ended up in the closet, with her bent at the waist and Brady taking her from behind for a quickie. That's not exactly the thing to be doing when she was so close to her due-date and a house full of guests arriving in the cold outdoors.

As she waddled toward the mudroom, she giggled at the thought of making out while her guests pondered on why no one was around to greet them. Behind her, she heard Brady's hurried footsteps as he rushed down the hallway and then up the stairs.

A moment later, JJ gazed out the frost-edged windows of the mudroom. Flurries whipped around the outdoor light fixtures and the path one of the guys had plowed earlier to the lake, already had a layer of fresh snow. Through the swirl of snowflakes, she made out the blinking lights of Blue's bush plane. Then the lights went out and she smiled as several dark shadows moved quickly out of the plane.

She counted them. Six. Happiness burst through her. They had all come! There had been an ulterior motive in inviting all the single people that she knew. Hmm, with Layla not coming, they now had three guys and three girls.

It was going to be fun watching how they interacted with each other and maybe she could see if she could maybe pair them up as couples.

She gasped as the baby gave her another swift punch. Man, she couldn't wait for the baby to arrive. She tenderly patted her swollen belly. Not tonight, sweetie. Not tonight.

Chapter Three

"BRACE YOURSELVES! IT'S really cold out here!" Blue shouted as she slid open the plane door and shivered against the onslaught of the frigid north wind and icy snowflakes that snapped against her face. She'd kept the interior nice and toasty for her passengers, so it was going to be a bit of a temperature shock when everyone got outside.

Usually, she wore a wool hat and many layers of clothing, but tonight was different. She'd dressed for a party and that included wearing a dress, leggings and not the warmest of an ankle length winter coat.

As she stood on the cleared ice, by the wing of her plane, she accepted the two bags filled with presents from Kelly and made sure the others were able to descend okay, pointing out to be careful of accumulated ice at the right side of the exit. The three men came out first. Being the gentlemen that they were, they assisted Kelly and Kaley. Blue had to stifle a laugh as the girls would have no problem climbing out. They were bush pilots like herself and worked at North Country Air. They were used to the harsh elements and hopping out of planes in all kinds of weather.

This evening, her co-workers looked different. The girls were dressed up with makeup galore and their hair all fancy with curls and they wore pretty dresses beneath their coats. It wasn't often the girls from North Country Air went to parties, but when JJ had invited them, they couldn't turn her down. She was the best cook ever and a joy to talk with and she lived all alone out here with three very sexy cowboys.

Despite the cold enveloping her, Blue felt a zip of heat rip through her as she remembered staying over at the ranch one stormy night.

She'd been sleeping in one of the upstairs bedrooms when she'd been awoken by odd noises. She'd climbed out of bed and gone down the stairs to investigate. She'd found JJ and Rafe and Brady in the living room. The three of them had been naked with JJ sandwiched between the two men. They'd been having sex.

At first, Blue had been shocked. Had almost gone back upstairs, embarrassed at intruding on their privacy. But the tangle of arms, legs, and bodies, not to mention their sultry moans and groans of pleasure, encouraged her to watch the caring way those two men had kissed and pleasured JJ.

After spying on that sensual ménage, she'd began to crave a loving relationship like that for herself, but she knew she could never have it. What JJ had, was special. Something like that would never happen to Blue.

Besides, she had no time for men and dating. She had her young daughter to look after and a full-time job as a bush pilot. It was just the two of them, and that's the way she liked it. Ivy had been invited to come along to the party too, but Blue had left her with the sitter for the night. The sitter was a lovely elderly and lonely woman who enjoyed Ivy's company. Besides, Blue wanted to be selfish tonight, and just enjoy adult company.

The three men that had started a horse ranch business some miles from here had also been invited to the first annual Moose Ranch Christmas party, as JJ had stated in her invitation. The three guys were relatively new to Blue.

She'd met one or the other on several occasions when dropping off their monthly mail. Early this Spring, she'd flown them here to Moose Ranch to surprise Brady.

Mitch, was Brady's younger brother, and he looked a lot like Brady. He was kind and easygoing and liked to talk to her, but she didn't encourage him because she needed more time to get over what she'd experienced in her past with men.

Paul was a nice guy too. He liked to talk about his latest animal patients who weren't limited to the racehorses they were now housing on their ranch. Paul had a knack for finding injured animals in the forest and healing them. Currently he was tending to an injured elderly rabbit who it appeared had gotten into a fight with an owl and had somehow managed to escape its captor.

Then there was Daegen. She hadn't gotten more than ten words out of him since she'd known him. He was starting to look like a gruff mountain man, growing out his hair and having a beard and moustache. He was a quiet one. But that was okay. Everybody was different and lived in the world their own way.

"The ranch house sure does look pretty, doesn't it?" Kelly asked from beside her as they all gathered around and stared up the slope toward the ranch.

There was a trail of red and green lights that twinkled amidst the snowflakes and the lighting would make it easy to follow the path to the ranch.

"I love how they decorated the trees with so many pretty lights, but it is a shame there are no neighbors around to see the beauty of it," Kaley said.

"Hey! We're neighbors," Mitch chuckled.

"They did it for us, I'm sure. It's a nice warm welcome. I should have brought my camera," Paul replied.

Blue noted Paul smelled nice. He wore a delicate scent of cologne that she couldn't put a name to. The men were just as dressed up as the girls. They wore pressed pants, nice jackets and aside from Daegen, the other two men were clean-cut.

"Hey, where's Daegen going?" Blue asked when she spied him strolling away from the group and toward the area where she'd first touched down with the plane.

"Going to turn out the gas lanterns," Mitch explained. "No use burning fuel."

"We should go and help him," Kaley suggested.

"He's fine. He likes to be alone. He said for us to go on up without him," Mitch replied.

Blue hadn't heard the men talking, but she figured Mitch lived with the guy, so he must know him best.

"Okay. He can catch up, because I don't know about you, but I'm freezing!" Paul complained as he cupped his hands to his mouth and blew. White plumes of mist floated all around his face.

"Here, let me give you a hand with these," Mitch said as he grabbed the bags from Blue.

Blue was grateful and smiled as Paul waved his hand, urging them to follow him. They all moved quickly toward the ranch house.

It sure looked homey here and it was so quiet. The only thing she could hear was the crunch of freshly fallen snow beneath their feet and the frozen lake as it cracked off a couple of spooky gunshot-like sounds in the area where Daegan had headed. But Blue knew the ice wouldn't break. The lake was solid. The creepy noises were just the lake forming more ice.

A sense of wanting a place like this for her very own, washed over Blue. The little apartment where she and her daughter lived was noisy all day and all night due a busy traffic intersection nearby and there were plenty of loud tenants. But the lady who took care of Ivy was so reliable and so sweet, that moving away from her just wasn't an option at this time.

However, every time Blue came out this way, a longing for a quiet place like this for herself and for Ivy always grabbed a hold. She wanted a place where her daughter could run around in the fresh air and sunshine and swim and be happy and be free of dangerous traffic and savory characters.

As they drew closer to the ranch house, Blue noted spirals of smoke curling out of a couple of chimneys and buttery lights splashed from the first and second floor windows of the log cabin. The lights shone across the snow-covered yard illuminating a tall six-foot snowman wearing a scarf, a wool hat, sticks for arms, a carrot for the nose and some small stones for eyes and mouth.

From in front of her, Mitch laughed. "My bet is Brady built that snowman. He always liked making snow people."

Blue wondered if Mitch knew about JJ sleeping with more than one guy here at the ranch. She knew the baby was Brady's, because Kelly had told her, but Blue had never told anyone what she'd seen that one night with JJ, Brady, and Rafe.

An owl hooted from somewhere close making her jump. The forlorn sound of several continuous hoots sent a round of chills up Blue's spine. Such a spooky sound.

Soft murmurs of surprise rippled through the crowd.

"Shhh, everyone, he's up there," Paul whispered.

Blue noted to where Paul pointed. Not more than ten feet up, almost just above them, perched right on top of the laundry post beside the ranch house, sat a big owl. The light from an upstairs bedroom glared perfectly upon him, revealing its features.

It was a mostly medium grey color, with tufts of dark grey, plenty of dark rings around the eye area. It had a black chin and white patches that made it look like he wore a bow tie. It gazed down at them with small yellow eyes, seemingly undisturbed by them being here.

"It's so fluffy," Mitch observed.

"It's huge," Kelly murmured.

"I've never seen one before," Kaley said.

"It's a Great Grey. Canada's largest owl. We're very lucky to see one as they're very secretive. He must have a good hunting ground around here or he wouldn't be here," Paul explained.

The owl emitted another volley of hoots and to Blue's surprise, there came an answering bunch of hoots from somewhere deep in the surrounding forest.

"Must be his mate," Paul said.

They stood in the cold for what seemed like an eternity, watching the owl as it leisurely blinked down at them. Soon, the tip of Blue's nose began to get really cold, and her toes were freezing in her fancy boots. It was time to head inside.

She was about to make a move forward when she spied JJ in the mudroom window watching them. JJ waved to her and Blue waved back. Excitement burst through her.

"Hey, there's JJ!" Kaley shouted.

Upon her shout, the owl suddenly took flight. Large wings flapped noisily in the quietness of the night and then it was gone.

Everyone laughed and teased Kaley for scaring away the bird and then Blue led the way as they all strolled forward, happily waving to JJ.

Wreaths laden with pinecones and puffy red bows hung in the mudroom's frosted windows and tiny yellow fairy lights twinkled along several of the windowsills.

She looks gorgeous, Blue thought as she ascended the steps. JJ opened the door to welcome them inside, but Blue took hold of the door and shooed JJ inside. The last thing she needed was to get sick so close to her due date.

Wafts of delicious scents curled around Blue as she held open the door. Her mouth watered, and her tummy growled. Not only was she cold, she was hungry too!

As everyone entered the mudroom, Blue noted how beautifully JJ's hair shone beneath the lights and how fluffy it looked. Envy swept through her. When Blue had been pregnant with Ivy, her hair had fallen flat, and she'd been miserable with her large size. But JJ didn't appear to be in any discomfort as she greeted her guests.

"Man, it smells really good in here," Kelly said.

"Wow, you look great, JJ," Mitch complimented as he set the bags down and quickly helped Kaley off with her coat and then he removed his own. He hung the coats on hooks and then he rubbed his red hands.

"Oh, you're just saying that, so you can get an extra helping of dessert," JJ said with a laugh.

"You look absolutely smashing, JJ," Paul added as he assisted Kelly in removing her jacket and hung their coats up. Then as Blue stepped inside, Mitch helped her out of her coat too.

"I'm so glad you all could come. The turkey is ready. But first, everyone please give me a hug," she ordered.

JJ reached out and hugged each of them and then quickly instructed the group to head into the dining room and find their seats at the table.

A nice feeling of coming home bubbled inside of Blue as JJ turned her attention to Blue and gave her a warm embrace. JJ smelled so nice. Of flowers and spices. She had made such a lovely home here on the ranch, especially after the horror of being incarcerated in prison for so many years.

She looked healthy too. Her cheeks were pink and plump, and her brown eyes sparkled with happiness and the baby was riding very low. Blue sensed the baby would arrive probably right on or near the due date.

"I'm so glad you came," JJ said after she let go of Blue. Then she frowned and peeked out a window.

"But someone is missing. I counted six of you getting out of the plane. Where's Daegen?" she asked.

"He's coming in a minute. He's taking care of the lanterns."

JJ's frown turned upside down and she nodded. Then her mouth dropped open and she clutched her hands to her chest with surprise when she saw the two bags filled with presents where Mitch had placed them.

"Oh, what's this? You didn't have to, sweetie. I told you all to just to bring yourselves," JJ chastised.

"We wanted to, JJ. You've been so kind to invite us for dinner, we wanted to get you and the guys something. And a little something too for the baby from all of us. You can open the baby's present on Christmas Eve or Christmas morning, however you celebrate it."

"We do both," JJ laughed. "Thank you so much. You guys are so sweet, and the baby will be pleased."

"Oh! And I brought your monthly mail too. The letters and bills are at the bottom of one of the bags. There's a letter in there from Milena too."

JJ grabbed Blue by her hands and squeezed.

"Oh, Milena, the poor dear. Another Christmas in prison. I so miss her. I'll read her letter later. Thank you so much, Blue. I really appreciate the presents and the mail. What would we do without you delivering our mail?"

"No worries. There're a few people lining up for my job, if I decide to quit some day," Blue admitted.

"I hope that isn't for a very long time," JJ replied.

Blue hoped not too. She loved her mail route. Loved how happy the hermits on her route got when she delivered mail and their groceries and then the highs she got while flying. But having a place like JJ had sure would have been nice. For herself and especially for Ivy.

"Oh, sorry ladies, I forgot the presents," Mitch said as he suddenly strolled through the doorway into the mudroom and grabbed the bags.

"And the place is decorated so perfectly, JJ. Blue, wait until you see the giant Christmas tree! And where's my brother? And the other two heathens? Did they desert you?" Mitch said with a wink to Blue.

"They're getting ready. There's always work to be done and they came in late. Now let's get out of the mudroom and into the house. It's cold in here," JJ said as she ushered Mitch and Blue into the hallway toward the back of the house.

Suddenly Blue felt anything but cold. Just being here with friends had quickly warmed her up and for tonight there wasn't any other place she'd rather be, than here.

Chapter Four

BRADY INHALED A TORTURED breath as water sluiced over his body washing away the soap suds. He hadn't been kidding when he'd told JJ she was killing him in not being allowed to be with her. He understood why he couldn't, but hell, it didn't mean he wasn't frustrated. He missed pleasuring her, making love to her, and sinking his aching shaft deep inside her accepting warmth.

It hadn't helped when he'd gone into JJ's bedroom and then into her bathroom to find her flowery scent everywhere, even here in the shower. Brady gritted his teeth as he moved into a position where the water pummeled from the showerhead onto the ultra-sensitive length of his engorged shaft.

Yeah, sure, he should be rushing his ass out of here, getting dressed and then greeting their guests right alongside JJ. But after seeing her in that sexy dress, and being alone with her, he'd lost his self-control. Kissing her warm, welcoming lips, seeing her pillowy breasts, touching her, suckling her taut nipple, and then getting cut off from the pleasure he'd been enjoying. Well, hell, that kind of interruption really sucked. He was going to be selfish for just a little bit and get himself some much-needed relief.

At least then he could relax and enjoy the evening with friends. In the meantime...

His hands clenched tight around his erection, and he imagined JJ here with him. On her knees, her gaze dark and needy as she stared up at him. Her mouth was open while he swirled his cockhead against her trembling lips. Her hands were wrapped snug around the base of his shaft. Her hot tongue licking, lapping, and loving.

He dragged the steamy damp air into his lungs as she opened her mouth, and he slid inside. He gyrated as he began a quick piston. He moaned his satisfaction as her warm lips stretched over his shaft and her tongue forcefully dabbed an especially sensitive area on the underside and then she sucked hard on his jerking flesh, keeping a firm suction.

Brady panted as the pleasure ignited. He pumped his hands faster over his penis. Harder and faster. Gasped and then swallowed his moans as the sensual spasms sparked and quickly burst, exploding like blades of electricity through his shaft and slamming hard up into his belly and beyond.

He came on a strangled groan, jerking and bucking like an out-of-control stallion who'd gone too long without his mate.

Oh, man, JJ girl, I really miss this.

Rafe heard the voices drifting up from the first floor the instant he shut off the shower taps. At first, he figured maybe Brady, Dan and JJ were talking, but he quickly learned their guests had arrived. He heard Kelly's cheerful laughter, an answering laugh from Brady's brother, Mitch, and then other excited voices. He needed to hurry and join the party!

As fast as he could, he towel-dried himself, blow dried his hair and donned his nicely pressed and cleaned clothes that JJ had lain out on his bed sometime earlier when he and Brady and Dan had been clearing the ice for the arrival of their guests. This was the first Christmas party they were having since JJ had been here.

It had been JJ's suggestion to invite friends over for this get-together. He hadn't been so sure about the idea, because of the timing with the kid coming so soon, but she'd been so excited, so who was he to protest?

Besides, she'd done a fantastic job decorating the living room and kitchen area too. She'd strung garland intertwined with cute miniature

sparkling Christmas lights around the room. Had draped a long strand
of garland over the fireplace mantel too.

She'd even requisitioned some thin slabs of Styrofoam they'd had
left over from an insulation job from one of the shelters, and after
getting him to show her how to use the band saw in the barn, she'd
designed and then cut out pieces until they were shaped like giant
snowflakes. He'd hung the giant flakes throughout the first floor. He
had to admit, they sure did look nice.

After Rafe was fully clothed, he ran a comb through his hair,
slipped into the hallway and stopped as he met Brady coming out of JJ's
bedroom.

"Well, shit, mister. You clean up real nice," he complimented Brady
who was now clean shaven and not a strand of hair was out of place.

"You too, my man. Who are you trying to impress anyways?"

Rafe laughed at the teasing glint in Brady's eyes.

"Same lady as you are," he answered.

"Come on, my man. Let's be on our way. That sweet lady of ours is
holding down the fort while we sit up here and gab."

Rafe grinned as he followed Brady down the hall toward the
staircase. He liked this side of Brady. Happy, easygoing, and best of all,
Brady was alive.

The past few months had been fraught with worry about JJ flying
that plane and going missing that one time, Brady getting tetanus and
almost dying and now there was worry about the upcoming arrival of
the wee one to their untraditional family.

He'd been praying every night for the safe arrival of the baby. After
a year of hard work and worry, they deserved happiness. Loads of it.
And he, for one, was quite ready for it.

Shit! Dan thought as he stared at his ragged work clothes where
he'd hung them up on the hook just inside the bathroom door and
listened to the laughter of guests passing along the hallway as they
headed into the dining area. In his hurry to beat Brady into the

bathroom, he'd forgotten the clothes JJ had insisted he wear tonight. They were in his room. Upstairs!

Now what was he going to do? He'd look like Rudolph the red-nosed reindeer, all out of place, with the others probably all decked out in fancy clothes.

Maybe he could sneak by them and head up the stairs? But he doubted he could do it. The dining room was well within the field of vision of those stairs, and he'd get caught.

Dan quickly towel-dried himself, then grabbed the blow dryer and began to dry his hair. He pondered on how he could get out of this mess. He could scoot across the hallway to the other bedroom and find something in the closet to wear? But JJ would know, and he would probably suffer endless teasing afterwards for not being man enough to go upstairs and get on his proper Christmas attire.

A sudden knock had him turning off the blow dryer and glaring at the door.

"Hey, are you in there?" JJ's cheerful voice curled around him like a welcome embrace.

Hell, he didn't want her to know he'd forgotten his clothes. But suddenly the door opened and his clothes, nicely hung on hangers, were presented to him.

Laughter from the guests drifted into the bathroom as JJ slipped inside.

Her eyes widened, and she made a cute little O with her mouth as she spied his nakedness. If they didn't have a house full of guests, he'd be pulling her right into his arms, kissing her smack on her sweet lips, and making love to her right here.

"Don't think you're going to get out of wearing these so easily," she said. Her eyes smiled with amusement as she removed his wrinkled work clothing from the hook, tossed them into the nearby hamper and hung up the fresh clothing she'd brought in.

"And don't think you're going to get out of here, without one of these," he whispered.

Her flowery fragrance mixed with a nice spicy aroma made him ache for her. Suddenly he wanted to touch her fluffy hair and feel her quiver against his body as he kissed her. Impulsively he took one step forward, grabbed her by her waist and pulled her against him. He loved how her sweet baby belly pressed against him, and he enjoyed the surprised expression splash across her face as he lowered his head.

He heard her breath catch as he sipped at her trembling lips. She melted against him, and she moaned softly as he thrust his tongue into her mouth. His cock hardened at her moan, and he answered with an animalistic growl. Loud enough for her to hear but not loud enough for their guests.

Guests. Darn.

But she tasted so sweet, her mouth so soft. He wished he could thrust his fingers into her hair and feel the silky softness, but he didn't want to mess up her hairstyle. Didn't want to mess with her lipstick either. Well, that part was probably too late.

Reluctantly he broke the kiss. She was breathing hard, her cheeks pink.

Slowly he pulled away.

Man, she was the cutest thing he'd ever seen. He swore she looked more beautiful with every passing day. Pregnancy really did agree with her, and he didn't feel an ounce of jealousy that she carried another man's baby. It just felt so natural, and he thought of the baby as his own. Loved it so much just because the baby was a part of JJ and Brady.

"Damn, pretty lady, you do look good enough to devour," he whispered.

"Any other time, Dan and I'd be devouring *you*," she said.

He chuckled as she pulled out of his embrace. She took a quick glance into the mirror. He guessed to check her lipstick, but he'd been careful not to smudge it. Much. She caught him watching her as she wiped away a smudge and gave him a warning look.

"Don't take too long. The turkey is being carved by Brady as we speak, and I want you to get some too before it's all gone. Our guests are hungry."

"Not as hungry as I am," he growled. That sweet smile that lifted her lips assured him that she got his meaning, and he didn't mean food.

She opened the door and slipped back out in the hallway and then closed the door behind her, leaving him with a hard-on that he knew only JJ would be able to quench. Since she was unavailable for the next little while due to the baby, he would have to be content with her second-best attribute.

JJ's cooking.

Dan grabbed the clothes and quickly got dressed.

Dinner went wonderfully, and JJ had enjoyed it when everyone insisted, she sit down and be served. The girls and Brady made sure everyone had enough helpings on each of their plates, and JJ was grateful for them taking over as it had been a long day. Her feet were sore, her back ached and every once in a while, the baby would give her a good punch. But she kept her discomfort hidden. She wanted them all to have a great time and truth be told on the most part, she was able to enjoy herself by watching her guests interact with each other.

They all seemed genuinely happy, including Daegan who had eventually joined them. She couldn't see any romantic sparks happening between any of them though. They just seemed like friends. Laughing, joking, and eating.

During dinner she caught Brady, or Dan or Rafe watching her with tender expressions and warmth would curl through her. *This* is what she wanted for her friends. She wanted to see *that* look of love that the guys gave her in one of the other men's eyes for one of the girls.

But it did not happen.

Oh dear, maybe she was just asking for too much having another romance, besides hers, to start right here on Moose Ranch?

After dinner, to her surprise, her guests paired off. Mitch and Blue hooked up to wash the dishes and Kelly and Paul volunteered to serve coffee, Christmas cake and the gingerbread cookies she had baked.

Even Daegen and Kaley were speaking in hushed tones. She caught them discussing their pilot experiences. Hmm, they had something in common.

With coffee and dessert finished, the girls asked JJ to see the nursery and she was happy to oblige and led them upstairs. She'd decorated the nursery walls in delicate yellow and blue toned wallpaper. Online, they had ordered white furniture; a crib, bookshelf, toybox and a change table which had come weeks ago.

The girls gushed over JJ's homemade white lace curtains and the cute colorful handsewn alphabet letters she'd made and then hung on various areas on the walls. She appreciated their compliments, and her happiness made her forget just for a few minutes, about her anxiety on soon becoming a mom.

Awhile later, they returned to the main floor, and joined the six men in the living room who were in deep conversation about their ranches. Soon their discussions turned into compliments about their pretty Christmas tree and JJ beamed with pride as she gazed at the tree that her cowboys and herself had decorated.

Yes, that tree did look spectacular, especially with the backdrop of an ice-frosted living room window and the nearby orange flames that flickered boldly in the stone fireplace.

Suddenly the group broke out into a cheerful string of Christmas carols. They sang traditional songs such as I'll be Home for Christmas, Jingle Bells and many others.

As JJ sang along with the chorus, she realized the baby had stopped being restless and was now quiet, allowing JJ to fully relax. She still chuckled to herself off and on at finding Dan, nude and looking quite guilty as sin as she'd brought his clothes to him in the bathroom. She remembered the shock coursing through her as she'd suddenly remembered that Dan wouldn't have his clothing in that bathroom.

Once Rafe and Brady had shown up, she'd instructed Brady to carve the turkey and then she'd discreetly excused herself and headed upstairs to retrieve Dan's clothing. She wasn't sure if anyone saw her bringing the clothes down, for if they did, no one said anything. So maybe Dan would be off the hook in the teasing department.

When the singing came to an end, Kaley and Daegen offered to serve everyone more coffee and more dessert. JJ couldn't help but laugh. She was surprised that there was still room in everyone after all the food they had stuffed away at dinner. But she was thrilled with their continued compliments about her cooking and her baking and grateful at her forethought of baking shortbread cookies, just in case. Well, those cookies came in quite handy now.

"So, Blue, have you given any more thought about that sheep ranch you once mentioned you'd like to maybe get started on? I just wanted to let you know that I haven't forgotten, and I am still keeping an eye out for something with appropriate grazing areas for the sheep," Dan blurted from beside JJ.

Everyone's gaze snapped to Blue and she looked a bit embarrassed at having everyone's attention to her.

"You want to start a sheep ranch?" Kaley asked.

"When did this happen?" Kelly questioned.

"Oops, you haven't mentioned it to anyone? Maybe I shouldn't have said anything?" Dan replied.

Blue shook her head. "It's okay, Dan. Yes, I am still thinking about it. I just haven't had the time to do any snooping around myself. And with my daughter...well, actually she's two now and quite a handful with her getting into everything."

"I can babysit her, Blue, if you need to look around for possible places," JJ offered.

"And I can babysit too. You know how much I love Ivy. Oh, guys she is so cute," Kelly gushed.

"I can volunteer for babysitting duty too, Blue. Just ask," Kaley said as she leaned forward. It appeared all the girls were quite interested in Blue's idea.

"There you go, Blue. No more excuses," Kaley said with a wink. "If it is something you want to do, then you should go for it."

Blue smiled and JJ could see the twinkle of excitement in Blue's eyes. JJ recognized that look. It was the same kind of expression she'd seen in the mirror when JJ had finally decided that despite her own mental health issues, she would learn to fly a bush plane.

The men, until now, had remained quiet.

Mitch was the first to break the silence.

"Living out here in the wilderness on your own with a little one, would be a lot of hard work. I should know about children..." Mitch gave a nod to Paul and then to Daegen.

"Hey! Not funny!" Paul said with a laugh as he got Mitch's meaning that Paul and Daegen were kids.

Daegen picked up a pillow and plowed it into Mitch's face. Mitch grabbed the cushion and pressed it to his belly and howled with laughter.

JJ smiled at their easygoing manner.

Even Brady got in on the action from where he sat beside Mitch on the sofa. He got up, curled his elbow around Mitch's neck and squeezed. She hoped Brady was embracing him gently because she didn't want any corpses in the living room.

"Hey! Quit making fun of your friends," Brady complained.

Mitch's face grew red as he continued to laugh. Alarm raced through JJ.

"Brady, you'll hurt him," she gasped.

Brady caught JJ's gaze and winked.

"His face always does that when he laughs. You should have seen him when we were kids and something sad was going on with one of my brothers or sisters. Mom or dad would only have to get Mitch laughing and everyone one would join in."

JJ looked around at the group and to her surprise they were all laughing too. She was the only one who was concerned.

Oh boy, she had to loosen up! She wanted to have fun too!

Sure enough, Mitch's deep belly laugh rocked through JJ and before long, she was brushing away tears and holding her sweet baby belly.

"You know, Blue," Rafe said after the laughter finally died away. "When you get that ranch, give Brady's sister, Jenna, a call. She can hook you up with a cowboy or two to help you out at the ranch. She's got that Cowboys Online business that she runs. Help through her organization is less expensive because of the applicant's circumstances, and Jenna does a great vetting job."

Rafe looked over at JJ and the warmth shining in his eyes for her, made warmth and happiness bubble up inside of her.

"Although we asked for cowboys, we got JJ and she's the best cowgirl we could ever have asked for," Rafe said softly. "I don't know how Jenna knew it, but somehow she knew JJ belonged with us."

The group had grown quiet now and suddenly all eyes were on JJ.

Oh dear, she could feel her cheeks warming up. Did they know she was sleeping with all three of her sexy cowboys?

"Hey, you're embarrassing my baby mamma," Brady said as he let Mitch go and gave JJ an endearing grin.

"Let's get back to the topic about a possible ranch for Blue," Paul replied.

Thankfully, the focus went back to Blue, and everyone began discussing her avenues for achieving her goals, that is, if she did decide to try her hand at ranching.

Later, the topic of Christmas presents came up. Rafe suggested that maybe they should open the presents their guests had brought? But their guests wouldn't allow it, stating presents would only be opened at Christmas time.

Then suddenly JJ felt tired. It had been a long day and tonight had turned out even better than she had hoped. She gazed over at the wall clock and was stunned to discover the time was one a.m.

How was that possible? It felt as if they had just had supper at six and now it was so late. No wonder she was tired. She hid a yawn by covering her mouth with the back of her hand.

"Someone needs to be tucked into bed," Brady suddenly said as she caught his knowing gaze.

Man! Nothing gets by him.

There came a round of gasps and comments about how fast the time was flying when one was having fun. Despite JJ, Rafe, Dan, and Brady insisting they all spend the night, the happy six said they would carry on with the party on the plane and began singing more Christmas songs as they headed down the hallway to put on their coats.

In the mudroom, JJ gave them all cookie tins of Christmas cake and other cookies that she had put together for each of them to take home. Then came goodbye hugs and Brady, Dan and Rafe shook hands with the men and gave the women hugs, thanking them all for coming. After calling out a final round of goodbyes, JJ, Rafe, Brady, and Dan watched the six people leave the warmth of the building. Cold air blasted into the mudroom and Rafe quickly closed the door after the last of the group left the building.

The guys scraped circles into the frost that laced the windows allowing them to see outside. When the departing guests' laughter rang into the mudroom, happiness surged in JJ's heart. Wow, they all had had a lovely time and they had gotten to know one another.

Thankfully, the snow had stopped falling, and a full moon shone bright and white, high in the black sky, allowing JJ to see the plane on the lake. The newly fallen snow sparkled like tons of diamonds had been spilled everywhere and she watched as Blue, Kelly and Kaley did a circle safety check of the plane and then everyone climbed inside.

The red and green navigation lights near the edges of the wing tips flashed on. Other lights on various parts of the plane followed and she could also hear the roar of the engine. She felt that familiar yearning to go up into the sky in her own plane as she watched the plane start forward. That desire of freedom flying had only grown with every passing day since she'd been grounded.

The plane picked up speed as it headed down the lake. The skis moved easily over the ice and moments later the plane was airborne, soaring into the moon-brightened sky. Then they were gone and today suddenly seemed as if it had just been a lovely dream.

"This was fun," Dan said from behind her. He swept his hand against her lower back as they continued to stand at the door window of the mudroom.

JJ leaned against him and inhaled softly. Dan smelled nice. Of pine and a hint of wood smoke, probably because he'd been tossing pine logs into the fireplace all evening long. She felt peaceful and loved in the gentle caring way he curled against her back and snuggled his bristly cheek against her cheek.

A string of hoots from an owl snapped through the quietness and JJ laughed as she remembered the excitement of everyone when they'd told her they'd seen the elusive Great Grey owl sitting on her laundry post.

"I think they enjoyed themselves," she said with a grin.

"They sure did. We'll clean up everywhere, and Dan, you tuck JJ into bed," Brady ordered.

"And make sure she gets lots of sleep," Rafe said from behind her.

It was Dan's turn sleeping with JJ tonight and she knew by the way his eyelids drooped ever so slightly, that sleep was all the two of them, plus baby, would be getting.

Yes, it had been a wonderful party and JJ knew that she had just started a tradition here at Moose Ranch. Plans were already forming in her mind about next year's party.

She could hardly wait!

Chapter Five

THE NEXT DAY JJ HAD little problem getting back into her regular routine. Especially since she'd had a such great night's sleep spooned around Dan's ultra-warm body. Despite the nagging little backache that seemed constant now, she felt well-rested and upon stumbling out of bed, having a shower, and then getting dressed, she discovered all three men had already headed out for work, leaving her a note of each of their exact locations.

They'd also left her a generous helping of scrambled eggs and sausages that only needed to be warmed up in the microwave. All the dishes, pots and pans had been washed and put away and the stove and countertops gleamed with cleanliness. No one would have guessed they'd had such a large gathering last night because Brady and Dan had done an excellent job in cleaning up and freezing the leftovers from dinner. Not that there had been much left over, but today she would make them some hearty turkey soup using the bones and some meat and she would add some of their garden vegetables that were stored in the cool cellar.

As she sat at the dining table, drinking her second cup of coffee, her gaze drew to the sunshine flooding into the living room and over their cute, huge Christmas tree. She remembered the first Christmas she'd spent here at the ranch and a sudden burst of heat flooded her cheeks.

Oh my, she had been bold back then, hadn't she? Taking turns sleeping with three men and not feeling shame. Everything had happened so naturally, and she'd just gone with her feelings in loving them and having them make love to her. Then on Christmas day, she'd experienced her first ménage and she'd known that she didn't want to live any other way than to be here with the three of them.

Now she was having a baby of her very own. She squealed happily and hugged her belly and a wonderful inner affection for her baby flooded her. She closed her eyes and just listened to the quietness of the ranch house. The gentle tic toc of the wall clock, her quiet breathing, and the chatter of a squirrel from somewhere outside the kitchen window.

I am having a baby.

It was just all surreal. She couldn't wait to meet her child. Although she had been talking to her baby over the months, she couldn't help wondering in all the time if she'd be a girl? Or a boy? Would he or she be healthy? And how in the world was she going to be able to keep her anxiety under control if something bad ever happened to her baby? A burst of panic snapped into her peace and JJ forced herself to control her breathing.

Okay, calm down. This not the time for a panic attack.

JJ shook her head. As if she could control her attacks all of the time. Sometimes they just happened, and she had to deal with them. But right now, housework and cooking needed to be done and that's when she remembered the letter Blue had mentioned. The one from Milena.

A moment later, JJ was rummaging through the presents and drew out the bundle of bills and letters that Blue had said was tucked at the bottom of one of the bags. She slumped onto the lounge chair in the living room and quickly sorted the bills from the letters, setting them into different piles on the coffee table. There were bills for feed, medical supplies for the cattle, parts for the tractors and atvs, other invoices and then a statement for a good amount of money that had been deposited into the business bank account. Money that the guys had been waiting for from the largest purchaser of their cattle. There was going to be some celebrating in the ranch house tonight, she was sure.

There also were letters and what she figured where Christmas cards from family and friends to Brady, Dan, and Rafe and the one letter from Milena to JJ.

Brady had put in a call to his sister, Jenna, requesting Milena as help over the Christmas holidays and to assist JJ with the baby, but Jenna had informed them that the programs the convicts participated in would not allow an ex-con to be near a baby. Since Milena was the only woman JJ wanted here with her as help, JJ had dropped the idea and decided she would care for the baby herself and carry on with household chores on her own. Other mothers did it and so could she.

The guys, thankfully had not argued with her decision. Not too much anyway.

As she held Milena's letter, JJ gazed up at the kitchen windowsill. A lovely gold rock sparkled there in the sunshine. The rock had been a present from Milena on her last day here.

She still remembered the words Milena had said to her.

You are precious just like gold. You are tough and beautiful. I want you to think of me whenever you look at this rock. Remember me, JJ because I will never forget you. The first chance I get, I'll come and visit.

The return address on the letter was from the penitentiary where Milena currently resided. Sadness clutched at JJ. Milena still had a few years left on her sentence unless Jenna's Cowboys Online program was able to place her somewhere just as JJ had been placed here.

Damn! Milena *was* a good person, despite her troubled past. JJ had experienced her caring nature firsthand while they'd been in the same prison.

JJ shook the memories away. No, she didn't want to think about her years of incarceration. It always brought her into a bad moody state, and she didn't want to do that to her baby. JJ ripped open the envelope and withdrew the single sheet of white lined paper.

She smiled as she recognized Milena's feminine handwriting. The letter was dated two weeks ago.

As she began to read, she could almost feel Milena's warm embrace envelope her.

Merry Christmas to Moose Ranch! And especially to you, dear Jennifer Jane and to your beautiful coming soon baby.

Have you picked a name? Will s/he be a boy? Or a girl? Or maybe you'll be surprised by twins?

JJ laughed out loud at that last question.

Oh no, one baby at a time for her. Thank you very much.

Hey, don't laugh. Doctors aren't always right and sometimes mothers are surprised. Sorry I haven't written but I ended up in solitary when I got back to prison.

Solitary! Milena? No way. Concern gripped JJ. She continued to read.

After experiencing the peace and quiet over at your ranch, I couldn't get used to the noise of the inmates. So, I finally got myself into some minor trouble. Picked a fight with an inmate and well, I got solitary and I loved it.

JJ shook her head and couldn't believe what Milena was telling her. When she'd been here, she'd told JJ that the quietness of the ranch and surroundings had just about drove her crazy.

No worries. I am back in general population and back to being a good little inmate, so I am sending you, Brady, Rafe, Dan, and your sweet baby, best wishes for a Merry Christmas and a Happy New Year!

Until we meet again, I send you many hugs!

Always,

Milena

JJ frowned as she read the letter a couple more times and then slid it back into the envelope. Why did life have to be so unfair? Why did nice people do such bad things and have to be locked away for so long? And why did some bad people manage to stay out of prison?

Then JJ brightened at her next thought. Maybe Milena would get lucky just like JJ had? Maybe God was putting Milena through this brutality, so she would appreciate something better that came her way in the future?

JJ squared her shoulders and nodded. She had to remain positive that Milena would some day get her happily ever after too. In the meantime, she needed to get moving. Household chores needed to be done and she had to get started on gathering the items for tonight's meal because her men would be very hungry when they came home for supper.

The next few days flew past so quickly that before JJ knew it, it was Christmas Eve evening and as she removed a roast from the oven, that weird little pain that had been niggling at her lower back over the past week, suddenly grew into a wicked spasm that had her gasping from the intensity.

Oh shoot! This is a hell of a time to throw out my back.

"JJ? What's wrong?" Dan asked as he strolled into the kitchen and caught her grimacing and pressing her hand to the small of her back. The last three days, the guys had started taking turns staying closer to the ranch house. JJ had told them she was fine but secretly she was grateful not to be alone because her anxiety was starting to climb. But she hid it from the men. She didn't want to stress them out. They had enough worries with all the work they had with the ranch.

Today had been Dan's turn to stay close and she was thankful he'd spent the day doing chores in the barn, cutting firewood out near the sawmill, and he'd also helped her with dusting and vacuuming this morning.

"I pulled a muscle. I'm sure it will be fine. Just remove the roast and set it on the counter, would you?" she asked. She'd left the pot sitting on the rack and the oven was wide open letting out all the heat.

"Sure thing, baby. Then we'll pack some ice onto your back. Man, I told you to call me when you wanted that roast out. You shouldn't be lifting anything," he chastised.

JJ nodded numbly as the pain suddenly began to radiate into her front.

"Oh," she cried out as panic snapped through her and she clutched her tummy. Had something happened to the baby?

Dan frowned and quickly moved to stand beside her.

"What's the matter? You don't look so good. Is the baby coming?"

Confusion gripped her. The baby. Was the baby coming? Maybe she hadn't pulled a muscle in her back? Or maybe she had and now the baby wanted out?

Her hands shook as she stared down at them. The pain ebbed away, and JJ breathed a sigh of relief.

"Maybe a false alarm?" she answered.

Please be a false alarm.

Her panic edged up a notch. Oh Lord, she wasn't ready to give birth.

Oh, what have I done? I can't take care of a wee helpless baby out here in the middle of nowhere.

"Just sit down and breathe like the online Lamaze program showed us. Remember what we learned?" Dan replied as he slid his hand against her lower back and guided her to a dining room chair. He didn't appear to be stressed out at all that she might be going into labor.

Boy, at this point, she wished he were in her position, and she was a guy who couldn't get pregnant!

"And remember what Layla said?" he asked as he helped her sit down.

JJ shook her head. At this second, she couldn't remember anything the midwife had told her. She couldn't remember anything about anything!

"False contractions are quite common in the last month of pregnancy, especially if you are under a lot of stress and doing plenty of physical activity. And you've had both because of the party you threw and refusing to slow down and not wanting hired help around the house, am I right?"

Oh no, she didn't want to blame this on the beautiful Christmas party she had thrown.

"I think it was just a muscle spasm," she reassured him. *Or maybe not?* Had she been crazy asking Brady to get her pregnant? What in the world had she been thinking?

She tried to remember how those breathing exercises went. Her mind was blank. Uneasiness snapped through her like a live wire. She couldn't remember anything she'd learned.

"Oh, oh, I recognize that look. Don't panic, sweetheart. I'm here," Dan reassured in a soft voice that, to her amazement, soothed her rattled nerves. He took her hands into his palms and squeezed her fingers gently.

"Everything is going to be fine," he whispered. She gazed into his green eyes. They reminded her of the forest trees in summertime. Oh! How she wished it were summer right now and the baby was here, happy, and healthy.

"I don't think I can do this, Dan?" she confessed. Thick emotions clutched at her chest and tears bubbled up in her eyes, blurring Dan from her view.

To her surprise, he burst out in laughter. He let go of her hands, and then brushed the pads of his calloused thumbs against her cheeks, wiping away the tears.

"I think it's a little bit too late to be thinking that, JJ. Ready or not, the baby is coming one of these days. Honey, do you feel any more pain?" he asked.

He smiled reassuringly at her and waited for her to answer.

She shook her head. There was no pain anywhere. Not even that odd one in her back where she figured the baby had been pressing his or her feet the last few days.

"Good, good. Then it was just a false contraction or muscle spasm. Did you want ice?"

"No, it'll just make me cold. I'm fine." *Yeah, right.* She felt like a beluga whale. Discomfort and anxiety oozed out of her, and she was telling him she was okay. She needed to have her head examined. She needed to get out of this awkward big body and back into her own.

Dan grinned and nodded. He wiped some more of her tears away and then stood.

"Stay there and relax while I carve up the roast."

"You don't have to do that, Dan." It was her job. She needed to keep busy. To keep distracted or she might start to really panic.

"Anything for you, sweetheart. And if you want to lay down on the sofa, and take a load off, maybe even a nap, while I set the table, it might help prevent another spasm."

"I'll stay here and watch my sexy man slave do housework," she teased.

Because she was suddenly pain free, she felt better and even in a playful mood now that hopefully she wasn't going into labor. Tomorrow was Christmas. It was her due date, but according to her research, that date was just an estimate. The baby could come earlier or later.

"Sexy man slave, am I?" Dan chuckled as he began carving the roast. "And you my dear, are you my sexy woman boss, holder of my heart and future mother of my babies?"

It was JJ's turn to laugh. "Please, let me get this one out okay, and then we can talk in like maybe ten years?"

Dan looked over his shoulder and did a cute eyebrow wiggle. "In ten years, we'll have plenty of kids running around here and you'll be the perfect mother, just like you are the perfect woman."

His compliments sent heat into her cheeks. He was such a sweet man. She was so lucky to have him. Best of all, her baby would feel so loved by all three dads and would never experience not having a father around. Nor would the baby ever be physically abused or scared like she had been by her stepfather and stepbrother.

Despite her fears of having to go through the pain of birthing any day now, JJ sensed she was the luckiest woman in the world and...her tummy growled. She realized she was hungry. Hopefully, that was a good sign, and she would have a bit more time to get used to the idea of becoming a mother.

JJ shook her head.

Dufus, you've had many months to get used to the idea. If you haven't by now, you never will.

She settled into watching Dan work. He whistled softly while he grabbed the oven mitts. She liked the way his jeans hugged his curvy ass. Loved the muscles that bunched in his bare arms as he carved the roast beef.

A couple of minutes later, he tucked the pan back into the stove to let it cook for a little while longer. Now, the only thing missing was his cowboy hat. Any other time, she'd be plopping it onto his head and demand he make love to her right here on the dining room table.

Yep, he was a sexy man slave. And he was all *hers*.

Christmas morning

A not very nice pain tore through JJ, ripping her from a very deep sleep. She came awake on a gasp. At first, she thought maybe she was in labor. But then she sleepily figured she was dreaming that she'd gone into labor because when she'd awoke, there was little pain. She'd had a dream of going into labor a couple of times over the past weeks, so she wasn't fully alarmed, and her grogginess had her confused, allowing her to fall right back to sleep.

She remembered how the guys had been concerned about her at dinner when Dan broke the news to them of what had happened when she'd been taking the roast out of the oven.

Both Rafe and Brady had chastised her, making her feel guilty about maybe putting the baby in harm's way by trying to lift the roast. She'd sucked up their concern like a trooper, teasing the guys that they could punish her as much as they wanted after the baby arrived. Her comment had made all three of them groan sexy sounds that JJ loved.

Because they insisted she rest, Rafe had done the dishes while she'd lain on the sofa cradling her baby bump and feeling overwhelmed with affection for her unborn baby as she watched the friendly fire flickering in the hearth and listened to Brady and Dan play cards.

When Rafe joined them, the guys opened their personal mail that they'd saved until tonight and shared their letters by taking turns reading them out loud and sharing with her their Christmas cards from family and friends. All the holiday cards had included her name with the well wishes.

Although she hadn't met any of their families, except Brady's brother, Mitch, she felt as if she knew their families through their letters and phone calls she'd taken.

After the mail had been sorted and attended to, the men had sat cross legged on the carpet like three big kids and opened only the presents that her guests had brought over during the Christmas party. They would save the presents they had all gotten each other for Christmas morning.

The guys and girls had pitched in and bought Rafe, Brady and Dan, lovely fleece-lined hunting jackets. JJ had instantly noticed the theme.

The blue and black plaid one had gone to Brady, who had blue eyes. The green and black plaid one was for green-eyed Dan and the brown and black plaid jacket had been given to Rafe who had brown eyes. She would make sure to send them all thank you notes for their thoughtfulness.

When JJ opened her present from the group, she'd been thrilled to receive a red and black plaid wool-lined jacket with hoodie. They'd decided not to open the baby's present until he or she arrived.

The evening had been lovely and relaxing, the baby calm, allowing JJ's rattled nerves to settle again as they all made plans for the ranch over the upcoming year. They'd all turned in early, the guys insisting that JJ sleep in her own bed to ensure she had a good night sleep.

She had been sleeping soundly again...until another nasty pain ripped through her belly and back, making JJ cry out at its intensity.

An unfamiliar sound rocked Brady from a nice sex dream he'd been having about JJ. For a moment he didn't realize where he was until his bedroom rolled into focus. It was dark as he gazed at his alarm clock. He was surprised it was only midnight.

He smiled.

Christmas had arrived. This was going to be such a nice day. They would gather around the tree and open their presents. He couldn't wait until JJ saw what they'd gotten for her. Couldn't wait to hang that mistletoe he'd been wanting to put up for that party last week, but JJ had talked him out of it, saying she didn't want to make her guests uncomfortable.

And then with all the work that needed doing around the ranch, they'd forgotten to hang that mistletoe. But he would do it. First thing in the morning.

He resisted the urge to head over to JJ's room, wake her and give her a Merry Christmas kiss. He had this overwhelming urge to place his hand over her belly and say Christmas greetings to the miracle growing inside of her.

Man, he'd been a bundle of nerves thinking that he was going to become a father. He wondered if all dads were like that, or just him. He knew he would aspire to be like his old man who had been strict with them, but also full of love, understanding, patience and he had given all of them the freedom to do their own thing. Yeah, dad had been a really cool guy and Brady missed him like crazy, especially whenever he was alone with his thoughts and memories. Like now.

He inhaled deeply and stared up at the ceiling.

Merry Christmas, Dad. Merry Christmas, Mom. I'm going to be a dad. Wish you were here. I know you would love JJ and our baby so much.

His thoughts were shattered when he heard that sound again. The one that had woke him in the first place. Only this time it was much louder.

JJ?

Adrenalin pumped through him as he whipped aside the comforters and swung his stiff legs out of bed.

Damn legs! He knew he had to sit here for a moment because if he just got up and started walking, he might fall flat on his face. His stiff legs were from the lingering aftereffects of his bout with tetanus, but he also knew that moving them while he sat here would get them in tip top shape in a minute. So, he began to move them. Fast.

He wanted to call out to JJ. To reassure her that he was coming. But then he heard footsteps rushing down the hall. Heard Dan and Rafe speaking in low tones.

Thank God. The guys would get to her. It would allow him to get his legs working properly. He wondered if maybe she was having a false labor pain like Dan had explained he thought she might have had earlier before dinner. Or...a sliver of uneasiness unsettled him. Was JJ having the baby now?

Another cry and he knew without a doubt now it was from JJ. This one rattled right down to his very core. He didn't want her to be in pain. Didn't want her to suffer.

Suddenly his bedroom door burst open. The lights flicked on, and Brady shielded his eyes from the intensity.

"It's time. The baby is on the way. I'll call Layla, but I doubt she can make it in time," Rafe said. "JJ's contractions are already two minutes apart. JJ's been timing them for about fifteen minutes on her own because she didn't want to wake us up. She thought it was maybe false labor pains. Dan is checking her now. God, that woman is a trooper. Didn't want to wake us. Man! I cannot believe her."

Brady let Rafe's words roll over him. Two minutes apart. Close contractions were not supposed to be happening so fast. Both dread and excitement filled him.

Keep your cool, man. Keep your cool.

He opened his eyes and found Rafe still standing there in the doorway. He wore nothing but his underwear. He looked a bit pale and when their gazes met, Rafe smiled.

"Shit, Brady. You're about to become a dad."

Oh boy. For an instant he *knew* how JJ felt when she was having a panic attack. Overwhelming terror. Heart racing. The inability to think straight. A shitload of emotions he couldn't put a name to were all tumbling around inside him.

Then Rafe was gone, and Brady heard JJ cry out again. The awful sound tore through him like a tornado and broke him from his temporary paralysis. She needed him, and he wasn't going to wait here one second longer.

Ignoring the stiffness in his legs, he managed to stumble to the nearby chair where he'd lain out his clothes.

Man! His beautiful woman was having his baby! Now!

Chapter Six

"I NEED TO GET UP. I need to stand, Dan. I need to push. Oh, another pain is coming."

Dan cringed as JJ's face crunched up in pain. She cried out and her fingernails dug painfully into his palms as he held her hand. He'd already checked her to see what was happening. The water had just broken according to JJ and he could see that she was already fully dilated. It looked like the baby didn't want to wait much longer to get into this world.

"Oh God, it hurts!" she screeched. She clutched the bed's headboard with her other hand, her knuckles white. As she closed her eyes, she let go of the headboard and rolled forward like a shrimp as more pain grabbed hold of her.

"Rafe said you need to stay put right here in bed until he gets back. So how about you concentrate on your breathing? Yes? Breathe through the pain." Dan began to breathe in the same way they'd been taught through their online birthing classes. He hoped she'd join him, but her brown eyes shone with pain, and she nodded jerkily.

And she began to pant instead.

Oh great.

Perspiration blistered across her forehead and her bangs were wet. Her damp nightgown stuck to her full breasts and because the water had just broke, the sheets were wet. JJ was shivering too. He wasn't sure if it was from fright or if she was cold.

"Hey, baby, what's happening?" Brady said in a soothing voice from right behind Dan.

Thank God!

Dan looked up and found Brady staring down at JJ. He didn't look so good. He seemed pale and his concern for her made his brows furrow, making him look mean and nasty. Man, if Brady didn't loosen up, he was going to scare her.

"Brady, sit with JJ. Hold her hand. I have to get a fire going in the hearth and get it warm in here," Dan instructed. He needed to get busy, or he would go nuts. Seeing JJ like this was killing him.

As he and Brady traded places, JJ smiled with love at Brady and a wonderful warmth burst inside of Dan. He enjoyed the bond that Brady and JJ shared. It was always a joy to watch.

Reluctantly he left their side and got the fire up and popping in no time flat. Rafe had entered the room again and was throwing around orders for someone to get JJ a glass of cool water to rehydrate her, boil some water, grab clean sheets, a dry nightgown for JJ, sterilize shoe laces and scissors and for someone to go down to the lake and get the lanterns lit because Layla, the midwife, would be here in about an hour and she would need a well-lit runway for her plane.

Dan was impressed at how Brady handled JJ. He held her hands, brushing his thumbs over her fingers in comforting strokes and he spoke to her in hushed confident tones, just like he did with their Angus cows. And he even got her concentrating on her breathing.

Rafe and Dan usually saved Brady for the difficult cattle births. He had a tender touch and a calming voice, and both were coming in handy with JJ because she suddenly didn't appear anxious at all as she stared in an almost trance-like state at Brady. Her reaction to knowing she was having her baby right now was nothing in comparison as to what had happened before dinner when she'd experienced that back spasm. Her panic had scared Dan, but he'd kept his cool in front of her not wanting to add to her fear. Just like he was trying to do now. But inside, terror rushed through him. It wasn't every day that JJ was having a baby!

Since Brady was soothing JJ as they waited for the next contraction and Rafe was plumping up pillows behind JJ's back, Dan suddenly realized all the orders that Rafe had just spat out, were directed at him!

Shit! He needed to get his ass in gear. Now!

"How...how much longer is...going to go on for?" JJ gasped between the spasms of pain that pummeled her. She hadn't realized this kind of pain could even exist. It was awful! And her anxiety was in full swing too. Everything that she'd learned on how to avoid a panic attack, just wasn't working.

Fear was her constant companion and that she couldn't control her anxiety just added to it.

"Soon, baby, soon," Brady reassured as he held her waist tight while they paced up and down the upstairs hallway. Thankfully, the guys had finally let her out of bed. She didn't know why, but the urge to get up and pace had been so great, she'd been barely able to stand still enough to have Brady slip a fresh nightgown on her.

When he had first shown up, she'd been so happy to see him. She'd actually been able to relax for a few minutes. But the pain came back and the periods in between the contractions were shorter, and she was now in pain almost all the time and she wasn't happy to see Brady now.

It was his fault she was in this situation. She just wanted this over. Wanted her baby to be safe and cuddled in her arms.

I feel so helpless. Everything is out of my control.

"How long has it been?" she gasped as the pain twisted through her even harder.

"Two hours. Layla is just landing. She had trouble due to the high winds and because it's snowing again. She'll be up here in just a minute. The guys have gone down to get her."

Two hours? It seemed like forever! There was no way she could go through this for more hours or days like most women did. No way. Panic shot through her at being stuck inside this awful pain for days and she fought back the tears of anguish.

"Brady, I can't do this. I just can't," she sobbed.

"You can do it, baby mamma. Let's just keep walking. Do you still feel like walking?" Brady asked as she suddenly stopped. She just couldn't anymore. Something was different. It was way too heavy down there between her thighs.

"The baby is coming," she whispered.

Fear twisted through her like a knife. She didn't want the baby to fall out and hit the floor. Instincts told her to lay down and push. Now!

Brady must have sensed something too, for he lifted her easily into his arms and brought her into her room. She barely noticed how nice and warm it was in here compared to the coolness of the hallway. Barely noted the cheerful fire flickering in the hearth, the dim lit candles on a couple of shelves on her walls. The bed sheets had been changed too and she suspected the mattress turned over as the bed was warm as she climbed in. Everything looked so orderly, as if she hadn't been in here earlier freaking out because the baby was coming much faster than any of them had anticipated.

Yet nothing was in order. Her thoughts were in chaos, but thankfully her instincts were taking over. She went with them.

"I need to push," she gasped. "I'm scared, Brady."

"I know you are. Me too," he confessed as he sat on the edge of the bed beside her. He took her hands into his and began that sweet massage with his fingers that he had done earlier. Too bad his technique just wasn't working this time around.

That he was scared too was not what she wanted to hear at this moment. She needed her man strong and confident. And he had been. Until just this second when she realized he looked tired and concerned and he had new worry lines etching the sides of his mouth. Why hadn't she noticed those new lines before now?

Sympathy washed over her.

"Brady, I am so sorry to stress you out," she ground out between the spasms of pain.

Brady cursed softly, and he suddenly looked pissed off.

"No, hell, no. You are not stressing me, sweetness. Not at all. We're just not used to this baby making stuff. We'll be fine. We'll get used to it."

JJ tensed.

What? What did you mean by we'll get used to it? No way in hell am I going to do this again.

The urge to push just about overwhelmed her. She couldn't wait any longer.

"The baby is coming. I need to push, Brady."

"Hold off pushing for just a sec. I'm going to take a look. Brady suddenly said.

"Oh no you're not. Everybody out. Let me check on my patient," came Layla's stern voice as she suddenly hurried into JJ's bedroom with Rafe and Dan trailing her. She carried one of those black doctor bags and each of the guys carried a couple of large plastic bags filled with who knew what.

Layla instructed the men to place the bags onto the floor near the fireplace.

JJ wasn't sure if she was glad to see Layla or be pissed off that she dare order her men out of her bedroom. But right now, was not the time to dwell on it because like it or not, her baby was coming out!

"This was so not how I had envisioned the arrival of the baby," Rafe muttered as he stood beside Brady and Dan out in the hallway. Upon Layla's arrival and ordering them out, he suddenly felt like an intruder in his own home. Had it come down to it, he would have delivered the baby himself and truth be told he was a bit irritated that Layla had told him she wouldn't need all the boiled utensils that had been prepared. She'd brought her own sterilized instruments.

Huh, he had brought Blue's baby into the world without much of a problem. He could have done the same for JJ.

It wasn't that he didn't like Layla. He did like her. Well, kind of. She was a serious lady, and he might even call her a bit of a bitch, especially when he'd asked her plenty of questions about her training and experience upon their first meeting. She hadn't seemed to like questions about her past life before her schooling as a midwife. But he reserved judgement because he didn't know her well enough to put that label of bitch firmly on her. He felt sure that by morning he would know if she was one or not.

The instant he'd seen her a couple of months ago, when JJ had decided she wanted Layla as a midwife, based solely on references from the women pilots at North Country Air, Rafe had thought the woman was way too young. He would have preferred someone in their fifties, not someone who looked like she was in her mid-twenties, although she had reassured him that she was of age and quite capable of taking care of JJ through her labor.

He'd drilled Layla on her labor experience, and she'd said she was registered at the College of Midwives of Ontario after doing a four-year stint at Ryerson University. He'd called both places just to make sure she was legit. They confirmed she had attended Ryerson and graduated their Ontario Midwifery Education Programme with honors, and she was registered at the CMO. Her references checked out and she appeared to have plenty of work experience and—

Another cry from JJ sliced into Rafe. It felt as if a knife was twisting through his gut. Man, he didn't like this feeling of worry and empathy for her. He felt bad. Beside him, Brady cursed, and Dan mumbled something about needing a coffee. But Dan didn't make a move to head down to the kitchen to make some.

"How the hell long does it take for her to check on her patient?" Rafe asked. He swore he would give the woman five more minutes and then he was going in! He looked at his wristwatch. Only two thirty. It felt as if JJ had been in labor for days not just a little over three hours.

Or was it under three hours? He couldn't remember. Couldn't think straight.

Could only remember the shock and fear shooting through him when he'd heard JJ cry out in the middle of the night, rocking him from his sleep and then finding her panting up a storm in her bed as she struggled to get up.

"It's only been a few minutes, Rafe. You gotta, relax," Dan said.

"Who the hell can relax?" Rafe replied. He wanted to jump out the nearest window and run away, so he wouldn't have to hear JJ's cries of pain.

Brady was remaining very quiet as he stood in front of the closed door staring at the doorknob. He could just imagine what the man was thinking. Either that doorknob turns now or I'm going in with both guns blazing.

Hell, that's what *he* was thinking.

Another cry came from JJ. Rafe gasped. Dan tensed. Brady's hand went for that doorknob.

"Easy, Brady," Dan said as he gently settled a hand on Brady's wrist.

"Give the midwife some space," Dan continued. "She must be one tough chick to be able to fly through a wild windstorm with all that snow blowing out there. I'm surprised she saw the runway at all, so I don't think a baby coming into the world is going to faze her. She wouldn't be a midwife if she didn't know what to do and didn't at least like her job, right?"

Brady nodded solemnly. His stern gaze did not move from that doorknob.

Yep, he was too quiet.

"What if something is wrong with JJ? What if something is wrong with the baby?" Brady suddenly asked in a voice that was drenched with apprehension.

Shit. Brady was thinking the same thing as he was? Oh man, he didn't want his friend to have all this worry.

"Hey, man. Don't do the *what if* scenario. That's your worst enemy right now," Rafe reassured. He wanted his friend to be happy. Joyful at this blessed miraculous time. This was supposed to be a happy time, wasn't it?

"Rafe's right," Dan replied. "We need to send in positive vibes to both JJ and the baby, so they can feel our love."

"We need to get *in* there and then they can feel our love," Brady snapped.

Suddenly the door burst open, and the midwife stood there. She was removing purple surgical gloves and there was a stethoscope draped around her neck. She had removed her coat and wore what looked like green scrubs. She was a short lady with too much wind-tangled dark brown hair and yep, she still looked like a kid. Too young for this kind of job.

She didn't appear the least bit stressed or worried and Rafe wasn't sure if that was a good sign or not. Over confidence in any kind of job could be an enemy just as much as the *what if something bad happens* scenarios running through all their heads.

"She's doing good. Both her and the baby's vitals are good. JJ's blood pressure is just a bit too high, but that's expected. I also gave her a shot of sterile water into her back for her pain and she's got a Tens machine on her back for muscle spasms. She turned down an epidural, so I gave her some tips about dealing with the pain.

The baby is almost here. JJ said you men did a fine job in keeping her walking and the room warm and the bed clean. She wants all of you in here with her. Now, before you go inside, I want to make sure none of you are the passing out cold kind of men. And that you don't drop at the first sign of blood? I don't need to be stepping over bodies while I'm working."

She lifted her eyebrows and looked at Brady and then at Dan and then at himself. At first, he thought he sensed some sparkle of humor in her dark brown eyes, but then he realized she was deadly serious.

Are you fucking kidding us? We run a freaking ranch. We don't fold at a birth or at the first sign of blood.

"They'll be fine," Brady growled as he brushed past Layla and entered the bedroom.

Rafe had expected the midwife to be a bit ticked off at Brady for being so pushy, but she just smiled at Rafe and Dan, stepped aside, and waved her hand in a gesture for them to enter.

Okay, so maybe she wasn't a bitch after all, Rafe thought as he followed Dan inside. He was kind of glad she was here. Took some of the pressure off.

"Hey, pretty lady, how are you feeling?"

Brady's soft voice snapped through JJ's wail of pain, and she wanted to ask him how the hell did he think she was feeling while she was giving birth to a huge bowling ball. At least that's what if felt like. But she reined in her nastiness. Being a bad-mouthing mom was not the first thing she wanted her baby to hear.

She kept her eyes closed, blew out her breaths just like Layla had instructed and reached out a hand to Brady. When he curled his warm fingers around hers, she inhaled at his strength. It made her feel better. A bit, anyways.

"Are the guys here?" she asked. She didn't know why, but she didn't want to open her eyes. She just wanted to melt into the pain. Live with it. Use it to her advantage and visualize the baby struggling to get out of her.

Help the baby by relaxing as best you can, Layla had said. *Let the pain guide the baby out. The pain is normal. Your fear. Your anxiety. All normal.*

It is all normal, Layla had said. But it sure didn't feel like it.

"We're here," came Dan and Rafe's answers.

She smiled. She wanted them here with her. They were her family, and they all made her feel safe and loved.

"So, which one of you can give me a hand? Rafe? You said during our first meeting that you and JJ delivered a baby once. Can you assist me?" Layla suddenly asked.

"I'll do it," JJ heard Rafe reply as the pain continued to melt all around her. Oh, Lord, she was drowning in it.

"Okay, I've got her in position," Layla was saying. "All I want you to do, Rafe, is hand me what I ask for, okay? But first you need to wash your hands, then slip on a pair of gloves just like I am doing now, okay?"

"Yep, no problem." Rafe's voice sounded strong and confident.

Thank you, God, for bringing me such strong men into my life.

"Everything we need is right there on the little table I brought with me," Layla continued.

"Brady, stay with JJ. Guide her threw her pain. Dan, I want you to please bring me a mug of coffee. I smelled it on my way in, but my patients always come first. Now that I know Jennifer Jane and the baby are fine, I can have a cup. Steaming and just black, please, because I sure could use one, okay? And make it fast, the baby is almost here."

"I'm on it," Dan said. Then it grew quiet in the bedroom. All JJ could hear was Brady's quick breathing from beside her, the howling wind outside, the snow peppering the windowpanes and water gushing out of the faucet in the adjoining bathroom.

And herself whimpering because of the pain.

The mattress by her feet moved and she the sheets over her legs lifted.

"Wonderful," Layla whispered in a loving and reassuring voice that made JJ glad of her decision in having her as her midwife.

"Everything is going along perfectly, Jennifer Jane. Now I want you to start pushing when I say, and I want you to stop when I say, got it?"

JJ nodded. Despite the wave after wave of emotions that overwhelmed her and mingled with the pain, she began to sob. She just couldn't help herself. Her baby was almost here! But when Layla told her to push, JJ did exactly what she was told to do.

Dan's hands shook like a son of a bitch as he poured a steaming cup of black coffee for Layla. Awhile earlier, just before he'd gone down to place the lamps on the runway for her, he'd put on a fresh pot of coffee. Usually, the scent of coffee was welcome but this time, it didn't lift his spirits at all, especially when he could hear JJ's cries trail down the stairs and wrap around his neck like a hangman's noose.

The baby would be here soon, and he was a nervous wreck. How were they going to deal with having a baby around the ranch?

Oh boy, what was he thinking? They could deal with well over a thousand herd of Angus beef with barely a problem and he was afraid of a little itty-bitty baby? Lack of sleep did that to him. Made him think stupid thoughts.

He grabbed the coffee for Layla and headed for the stairs. Just as he reached the top, he heard nothing. There was utter and complete silence.

Oh, oh. Silence was not a good thing, was it? With dread swirling around Dan, he hurried forward and then breathed a sigh of relief as he entered the bedroom.

Layla sat on the bed, hunkered between JJ's thighs, a sheet hiding JJ's lifted legs from his view. Rafe sat on a chair beside the bed handing Layla a towel and Brady sat stiff as a board, his face pale as a ghost as he spoke softly to JJ, who lay with her eyes scrunched up tight. She clutched both of Brady's hands, her knuckles just as white as Brady's face. Perspiration matted her bangs, her neck and her chest and her face was red.

"Okay, JJ, one more push. Just one more...and we have her! She's out and she looks wonderful. Brady, would you like to do the honors of cutting the cord?"

Her. A girl. We have a baby girl!

"You have a baby girl," Layla announced cheerfully. Her announcement stunned JJ as she stared up at Brady. He had a look she'd never seen before on his face as he stared down to where he had just placed her baby on JJ's chest.

"She's beautiful," she heard Rafe whisper as he came around and gazed down at her and the baby.

"She looks like her mamma," Dan said and threw JJ a wink.

Everything seemed surreal. It had all happened so fast. One minute she'd been told to push, and the next minute Layla and Rafe were cleaning the baby and then handing her to Brady who had laid her on her chest.

And they were right. She was so beautiful. Perfect. She looked as sweet as a cherub, and as cute as a Christmas angel.

Emotions bombarded JJ and she just couldn't stop staring at her, nor could she stop hugging her.

Chapter Seven

"I'VE NEVER FELT THIS way before," Brady said in a hushed tone.

The two of them lay in Rafe's bed where Brady had carried her and the baby while the guys and Layla freshened everything up in her room.

Their daughter, who lay on JJ's chest, was wiggling around and making sweet little cooing noises. Layla had already shown JJ how to feed her, but the baby hadn't taken to her nipple yet. But Layla assured her that she would. In the meantime, there was a breast pump all ready to go on the nearby table, and sterilized bottles, if needed.

Laughter from downstairs rolled through the open doorway. Rafe and Dan had eventually taken Layla downstairs for another cup of coffee and JJ hoped they would feed her too. They'd promised to come back up a bit later, but JJ sensed they were giving Brady, herself, and their baby a little bonding time.

"I've never felt this way before either," JJ whispered as she watched her baby. Her heart twisted with so much love, that she wasn't sure she could handle the depth of this new emotion and darn it, she wanted to cry again.

Her daughter was just so adorable. She already had her blue eyes open, and she was looking around. JJ touched the tip of her finger to her small button nose. Then stroked along her velvety-soft chin and up along her bottom lip. The baby made a little suckling motion with her sweet mouth.

Emotions bubbled thick and raw, and JJ fought back another round of tears that seemed to be her constant companion since giving birth.

"Perfect nose. Sweet pink lips. Tiny little fingers. Man, I haven't seen such tiny little fingers before," Brady murmured as he slid his finger against their baby's palm.

To JJ's surprise the baby clutched his finger.

"She's got quite the grip!" Brady laughed and tried to pull his finger away, but she just held on tighter.

"Already daddy's sweet girl," JJ said softly.

"Have we decided on a name?" he asked. "I know we talked about it being our mothers' names..."

JJ shook her head. "Suddenly all the names we were thinking just don't fit her."

Brady chuckled.

"I was thinking the same thing. What does she look like to you?" he asked and the instant he asked the question, she knew.

"Christmas."

"Merry Christmas to you too, sweetie," he said. He leaned over and kissed her so delicately on her cheek that she swore her toes tingled.

"I mean she looks like Christmas. Her name. Chrissy for short."

When Brady didn't say anything, she gazed at him. There was a cute little tilt to his head as he studied Christmas. She really hoped he would go with that name.

"Christmas angel. Christmas miracle. Christmas Jane. C.J. for short," he said.

Oh my gosh, Christmas Jane. The names fit.

"Christmas Jane. C.J. for short. But will she have a problem being named after a winter holiday?" JJ asked as a niggle of doubt suddenly crept in about the name.

Brady shook his head. "I had an assistant at the law office and her name was Holly. I also knew a woman whose name was Angel. Those names are Christmas themed. And Chrissy or C.J. are available for her if she ever decides she doesn't want the name Christmas, especially in the summer."

JJ laughed and cuddled her wiggling bundle of softness closer and then spoke to the infant.

"I can just see me being mad at you one day and saying Christmas Jane! Stop bothering your brother!"

"Or your brothers. Or your sisters," Brady added, with a grin.

JJ smiled. Now that the pain of birth was almost forgotten, and Chrissy was snuggled safely in her arms, maybe she'd been too hasty in thinking of only having one kid? She'd only been mostly uncomfortable the last three or so weeks and some bad days with morning sickness. What was a few weeks of discomfort for a lifetime of joy?

"Yeah," JJ chuckled. She was already liking the idea of a sibling or two or three for C.J., maybe even a dog or a cat too?

"I think she's hungry now," Brady said. "She's trying to tug my finger up toward her mouth."

JJ laughed as she gazed at her sweet little princess. Sure enough the baby's mouth was doing all the things that Layla indicated meant she was hungry.

When JJ moved Christmas Jane closer to her breast, and nudged her nipple into the baby's mouth, the baby began to suck and to JJ's surprise, her milk had come in.

Having her baby at her bosom, knowing JJ was able to feed and nourish her, despite the uncomfortable tenderness in her nipple, was absolutely the best feeling in the world.

As JJ slept with the sleeping baby on her chest, Brady slipped out of bed and gazed down at them. His heart absolutely burst with love.

His family. His beautiful woman. His beautiful baby.

He had a family of his *own*.

Wow, this morning had been intense. It had never entered his mind that the baby would come so fast. But after Layla had learned from Dan about JJ experiencing back pains, she'd chastised them for not letting her know. How the hell was he supposed to know a woman could be in labor with a simple backache and not even know she was in labor?

But he understood JJ. She probably hadn't thought much of it, assuming it was still from that tumultuous plane landing she'd been involved in. Perhaps she had pushed through it all on her own, not wanting to bother anyone.

Damn, sometime, she was just too independent. He was going to put a stop to that. At least over the next week or so. Reluctantly, he left the bedside and slipped out of the bedroom. He needed to make some phone calls.

Layla finally allowed JJ to get up and out of bed that afternoon. By evening, Layla had left, informing JJ to take it easy and that she would be back in a couple of days to check in on them. In the meantime, JJ had to promise she would call the midwife, day, or night, if there were any worries at all.

JJ had promised. Her first concern from here on out was always going to be their baby. She knew that now and she would never put Christmas Jane in any kind of jeopardy. The first thing JJ did after Layla left, was bring Chrissy downstairs to see the Christmas tree.

It didn't matter that her daughter was busy sleeping while JJ gave her a tour of the house. She just wanted her baby to hear her voice and for her to know she was loved so much. After, Chrissy woke up and cried, Rafe helped JJ change her diapers and then JJ fed her again.

Dan had cooked a light meal for all of them and after supper, JJ insisted they lounge around the tree and open their presents.

This was the best Christmas ever, she thought as they lay Chrissy down on the couch. Nearby, a friendly fire flickered in the hearth. It was warm enough in the living room, but JJ had swaddled her in a soft beige blanket and placed a beige knit cap on her head.

Rafe, Dan, and Brady took turns sitting beside JJ and watching C.J. sleep. To her surprise, the usually loud cowboys, spoke in quiet tones as they opened their presents.

She watched each of her men. They'd barely had any sleep last night, but they didn't appear the least bit tired. All three wore bright smiles and cast JJ and the newborn so many adoring looks that made her heart so happy, despite her wanting to cry.

Soon, the floor was littered with colorful bandanas, work gloves, brand new steel-toed work boots for each of them, jeans, shirts for the summer and the winter and plenty of new long johns.

"Wow, awesome! JJ got me that ratchet set I'd been thinking on getting! How'd you know, baby?" Dan asked from his perch on the carpet as he gazed adoringly at the set of shiny tools.

"Kind of hard to miss when every time I walked into the office and saw you looking at the ratchet sets online on the computer."

Dan laughed. "Dead giveaway, eh?"

"Damn! You got me that portable fishing rod I was going to get this Spring. Thanks, JJ!" Rafe said as he began putting the fishing rod together.

"Looks like we have two other kids here, hey baby?" Brady snickered.

"Hey! Not nice!" Rafe said with a laugh.

Rafe grabbed another brightly wrapped present from under the tree and tossed it to Brady, who caught it easily.

"Come on, let your inner kid out to play. That one there is the last one from JJ," Rafe said.

"Alright, if you all insist," Brady said with a huge grin.

JJ smiled as he ripped his wrapping paper and surprise etched his face when he saw the gift.

"Woah, now this is something I've been toying with getting for years, JJ. We have so many sugar maple trees on the property. Thanks, sweetness." he said and gave her a sweet kiss that made JJ want to cry.

Oh great. She probably had the baby blues now.

Brady held up the large package containing a maple syrup tapping beginner's kit.

"It has a book that shows you how to tap the maple trees, there's sugar making tools and instructions on how to make maple syrup. I figure you can use the buckets in the barn to collect the liquid and we have tons of firewood to cook the syrup," JJ said as the guys hunkered in around Brady to inspect the kit more closely.

"Man, no more excuses, Brady," Rafe laughed and slapped Brady on his back.

"Now with a kid, you're going to want to give her something natural to eat for her sweet tooth," Dan said. He gave JJ a wink and a nod of approval.

"Thanks, JJ. This is going to be awesome taking Christmas out on the snowmobile and have her help me tap the trees," Brady replied. His eyes were full of cheer as he gazed down at their newborn daughter.

"We'll start a family tradition, right, sweet baby girl?" Brady asked the sleeping infant.

"Now it's your turn, JJ," Dan said and soon the guys were handing JJ the presents they had gotten for her.

JJ chastised them for getting her presents because they and Chrissy were all she needed for Christmas, but she had fun ripping the wrapping paper and opening boxes. The guys had given her much needed clothing; a new ski suit – thankfully not maternity, wool hats, mitts, gloves and even a couple of pairs of very warm looking knee-high winter boots.

They brought her jewelry; a gold bracelet, gold cowboy hat earrings, and of course she wouldn't let the cowboy earrings pass without teasing them that she'd be wearing those earrings when the time came again for intimacy. Layla had informed Brady and herself they should abstain from sex for at least six weeks.

But JJ didn't mind. She was unusually tired and weepy, and sex was the last thing on her mind.

When Brady suddenly disappeared for a few minutes and then came back carrying something large in his hands, JJ just about started to cry when he placed the item on the coffee table.

"Rafe, Dan, and I made it. It's a knotty pine baby cradle. We can keep it beside the bed until she's a little bigger. We carved it out by hand," he said.

"It's so beautiful," JJ whispered. She'd never seen such intricate work before. She reached out and ran her hands over the delicate raised swirls and designs that had been carved into the wood. She knew they were good with wood, but she'd had no idea they were such talented carvers too!

Rafe turned the cradle so she could see the outside headboard area. There were two deer carved into the wood. The deer were grazing on grass. Pine trees had been etched into the background and a creek ran through the meadow.

"Oh my gosh, I know where this meadow is," JJ laughed and clutched her hands to her chest. This place was one of her most favorite in the world!

"Thought you might," Rafe laughed. "Wasn't sure if it was appropriate on a baby cradle, but hey the kid doesn't have to know. I just thought it was a beautiful place."

"It is appropriate, and the carving is so stunning," she complimented. The three guys had made love to her one bright sunny afternoon in this meadow. It had been such a gorgeous place. Peaceful and pleasure filled.

Then Dan reached out and twisted the cradle around, so she could see the outside footboard.

"And I carved this part," Dan said, pride flowing through his voice.

"Oh my God! It's the ranch house!" JJ gushed. The design was intricate and showed off the two-story log cabin with chimneys, and the windows and even the birdhouse they had in front of the kitchen window.

"It's gorgeous, I can even see a face in an upstairs window. It's the nursery window!" JJ gasped.

"That would be the baby looking out the window. I know it doesn't look like her, but hey, we didn't know how she would look, right?" Dan chuckled.

"And the rest, Brady made," Rafe said. He brushed his fingers along the swirls and curls of carvings that swept along the sides.

"Hey, I can't draw worth a hill of beans, so I went with the designs," Brady replied. "Do you like it, Jennifer Jane?"

"Brady, the designs are absolutely creative, and you melded them in so perfectly with what Rafe and Dan carved. Everything matches and of course I love it! Group hug!!" she reached out and all her three men crouched in around her and she bundled all three of them close to her. Not an easy feat with three big guys.

"Gosh, how were you able to keep me from finding it?" JJ laughed.

"Well, we know you like to snoop for your presents," Brady replied.

JJ gasped in mock horror. True.

"So, we wrapped it inside a tarp and hid it in behind a bundle of hay on the second floor of the barn. Dan brought it in earlier and stashed it in the first-floor bedroom closet," Rafe said.

"Earlier, while you two were upstairs sleeping, we showed Layla the padding and stuff we bought for the cradle," Brady said. "She approved the safety of everything, so once the cradle warms up and we can get all the padding and blankets in place, we can use it whenever she's ready."

"Oh, wait a minute," Dan suddenly said. She caught him wink to Rafe and Brady. Then he stood and strolled out of the living room. A moment later, he reappeared, and JJ's mouth dropped open in surprise at what he carried.

"A rocking chair!" JJ couldn't believe it. She'd thought about getting one to put in the nursery but hadn't been able to decide on which kind.

As Dan placed the chair in front of her, she knew this was the chair she would have picked. It was solid and sturdy. It was even padded with a fluffy cushion.

"Hey! How come I wasn't let in on this gift for JJ," Brady complained.

Dan and Rafe chuckled.

"Because it is a surprise for the both of you," Dan replied.

"Yeah, you're the dad, so when duty calls, you'll be spending plenty of time in this chair rocking the baby too, right JJ?" Rafe asked as he gave Dan a playful nudge to his ribs.

"All of you are dads, so you'll all be bonding with her," she reminded. She wanted Rafe and Dan to feel like they belonged to Christmas too.

"Aw, shucks, sweetness. We hoped you'd think so." Dan took a seat near the baby and smiled down at her.

"I swear if she weren't sleeping, I'd be hugging this girl. She is the best-looking baby I've ever seen, and rest assured I will be fighting off any of her beaus with a shotgun in each hand when they come snooping around," Dan warned. His forest-green eyes blazed with protectiveness.

"I'm thinking when a potential suitor finds out she has three fathers, she won't be getting any boyfriends," JJ joked.

A chorus of laughter from the guys echoed through the living room.

Happiness gushed through her as she gazed at the endearing knotty pine rocking chair, then at the beautiful cradle and then to her sweet baby, Christmas Jane, who slept soundly and totally oblivious that she was the luckiest girl in the world in having three dads. This was all so wonderful, and she swore that at this moment she'd never felt happier in her life.

This was the best Christmas ever!

The next several weeks fly past so fast that JJ couldn't even think straight. She was tired all the time and emotionally all over the place.

According to her mid-wife being emotional was normal due to the hormones. Layla brought her up to speed about post-partum depression and to keep an eye out for it, but so far JJ felt only love for her baby and wanted to be near her and take care of her.

To her surprise, Kelly had come the day after Christmas and stayed for a week to help JJ run the ranch house. Brady had called her, and Kelly had dropped her life, taken vacation time owed to stay here with them.

She was a wonderful help. At first, JJ had been mad at Brady for interrupting Kelly's life, but then she'd accepted that yes, Brady was right. She needed the rest and the down time of not having to prepare meals and keep the house spic and span as she loved to do. It had allowed JJ to have precious time to bond with her daughter and to rest.

After Kelly left, to JJ's surprise, Kayley came and stayed with them for a few days. Once again, Brady had been behind it.

But she was grateful for their help. They had given her tips that made life after having a baby so much easier. Having Kelly and Kayley here eased her anxiety too and by the time Kayley had left, JJ felt her normal self again. Almost.

But Layla assured her that she would be back into the swing of things, sexually, in no time flat and JJ could hardly wait for that to happen.

It was about six weeks after Christmas Jane's birth, and the weather had turned exceptionally warm over the past two weeks, when JJ noticed she was truly feeling better.

She looked forward to waking up early, so she could have a nice hot shower and prepare breakfast for her cowboys. The days were also getting longer and brighter and happiness bubbled inside her as she spied brilliant-colored blue jays visiting the bird feeder outside the kitchen window. Even the dripping sounds of the snow melting off the roof, made her giddy.

But she knew the mild weather wouldn't last because this was just the traditional January thaw, a mild spell that happened almost every mid-winter, usually toward the end of January. Except this year, the thaw had lasted well into the second week of February and the sunny, spring-like weather was just what she needed to put that spark of wanting sex back into her.

Love welled as she gazed at her baby who lay in the cradle blinking up at her with sleepy eyes. Her baby was thriving. She was gaining weight, and she was such a happy little girl as she kicked her chubby legs and waved her pudgy arms around. She had the plumpest cheeks and JJ couldn't resist kissing them or lovingly pinching them every chance she got. Best of all her baby looked so much like Brady, with the same shade of dark brown hair and blue eyes.

She'd gone back to flying her plane too. She loved the freedom of soaring into the sky. The little time away from her routine, thanks to the guys who took turns to babysit for an hour or two every morning, seemed to help keep her anxiety at bay. But every once in a while, anxiety and worry niggled at her. So far though, she had managed to keep it under control by becoming aware of her thoughts and then trying to figure out what was truly bothering her.

Sometimes it was worry over why the baby was fussing so much that particular day. Other times, she realized she was thinking the *what if* scenario. What if she had another panic attack? What if something bad happened to her while she was flying her plane, and she couldn't come home and take care of C.J.? What if one of the guys didn't come home? What if...nothing bad happened and she'd made herself sick over nothing?

She allowed her mind to wander back to her plane. It always made her happy to think about how far she'd come since arriving here at Moose Ranch with her anxiety issues. Back then, the mere thought of flying in a plane had literally made her sick with panic. With hard work and in slowly changing the way she thought, she had overcome her crippling fears on the most part and had learned how to fly. How cool was that?

She was also helping the guys deliver the feed, by flying the plane low over the various meadows that were dotted with black and brown Angus cattle. The guys would push out from the plane the bales of hay and other nutrients the cattle required. The plane drops would cut their work time and allowed her men to come home to her at night.

She'd taken C.J, as the guys loved to call her, up with them in the plane too and JJ had kept the cockpit nice and warm for her baby. Christmas didn't seem to mind the rides. She didn't get airsick or fussy. However, she was quite fussy during the nights when everything was quiet, and JJ was thankful the guys took turns getting up for the baby, changing her, rocking her, and giving her a bottle of the breast milk she always prepared, so she could have a good night sleep.

Thanks to their help, her lovely yearnings to want to be with her three men was back almost full force. But she didn't tell them she was craving her cowboys. At least not yet. She would need a few more days to prepare herself. To get ready for what she knew she wanted, especially after being away from them for so long.

Chapter Eight

"Have you guys been back for long?" Brady said as he tugged off his gloves and joined Dan and Rafe in the barn's small office. The two men were huddled over the computer, the screen open with their order for various nutrient packets they needed for the cattle. Due to the exceptionally cold winter, they'd been supplying the cattle with more feed and nutrients than usual. They were starting to get low on those specialized packets and the time to order was now.

Thankfully, it was nice and warm in here, compliments of the propane fueled infrared heater tucked away in the corner.

"Got back about half an hour ago. Just doing the order. Give it a quick read and see if you agree with the amounts." Dan said.

Brady leaned over and checked and nodded his approval.

"Yep, I think that should do it," he said.

"Good. And now we hit send, and voila." Dan pushed the enter button and Brady sighed in relief.

He knew that by this month's end, the feed company they used would have what they needed and packed on small pallets to their specifications. When the order was ready, JJ would fly one of them and a lightweight forklift they had purchased for such occasions out to Thunder Bay. Their order would be ready at the airport, and they would load the skids onto the plane in such a way that the weight of the items was distributed evenly, and JJ could fly the plane with no problems.

"Yeah, and we did just as we planned," Rafe said. "We split up and checked the east section to make sure the last plane drop of food was successful. All the hale bales exploded on impact and the cattle are getting access to their feed and nutrients. Everything looks good. The creeks and rivers are flowing, and no sign of wolves."

"Good stuff," Brady said.

He'd been away all day on his snowmobile too, and with the days still being short, it had been dark and cold when he'd returned. He'd been out to the northern perimeter to look for wolf tracks and to check the snow-covered meadows with the older cattle. He would quickly bring Rafe and Dan up to date on his findings and then get into the ranch house to see JJ and Chrissy.

Every time he was away from them, he missed them like crazy and today was no exception. He especially loved the cute little smiles his kid gave him when she saw him, and he swore too that she was even trying to say the word daddy, although JJ insisted she was still too young to talk.

"Had to break open one of the creeks for the cattle to get access to water. Figured the warm weather would take care of it, but not that one creek that always freezes up. Maybe in the future if we get more extreme winters due to climate change, we keep the cattle out of that meadow. Too time consuming," Brady suggested.

"And it's a pain worrying about them not getting a good drink," he continued. "A fence was downed by a tree branch. Took care of it. A tree fell onto one of the shelters, but it's too big to do in one day. No significant damage that I could see to the building, so I left it for another day. I'll put it on our list of things to do. Everything else looked good on my run. And I haven't seen the wolves either."

"Good. That's four weeks now with no wolf sightings. Maybe our tactics in scaring the crap out of them with gunshots finally chased them off," Dan said.

"I bet the wolves headed south. With more snow than usual, it would be harder for them to get around and take down the beef," Rafe replied.

"And I for one am not complaining about this mild weather we've been having lately. It's been nice to have a warm ass while working outdoors," Dan said with a chuckle.

"Hate to rain on your parade, my man, but I heard on the satellite radio last night that today was the last nice day. Going to be back to frigid again overnight and colder days. They figure it will stay cold well into April," Rafe said.

"I'm sure I can help keep you boys warm."

The instant Brady heard JJ's sexy-toned voice drift into the barn office, he knew she was back to her old self again. It had been torture seeing her tired and not her usual cheerful self since the baby had been born. With them not being able to do anything about it, except as Layla had instructed, be patient and help JJ out as much as possible and just wait until her hormones righted themselves, it was frustrating not to be able to do more for her. Lately though, he'd noticed she was starting to hum again while she cooked and that extra sparkle in her sweet laughter when one of them told her a joke, was coming back.

At her voice, all three of them turned to the open office doorway, but she wasn't there.

"Where is she? Sounded like she was right here?" Dan questioned.

"The baby monitor," Rafe suddenly whispered and nodded to the monitor that had been placed on a work shelf.

Shit. Why hadn't he noticed the baby monitor in here? JJ didn't come out here into the barn often, she was too busy with the baby and chores, so having a monitor out here meant she was up to something.

"The little vixen," Brady whispered as understanding dawned on him.

"Why don't you boys drop all your work attire and join me upstairs in my bedroom?" her voice echoed from the baby monitor.

"Drop our work attire?" Dan laughed. "Wonder what she means by that?"

Brady wasn't going to wait around for Dan to figure it out, and it appeared neither was Rafe, because the two of them practically had to squeeze past each other to get out the office doorway.

"Last one here, gets to tie me down," she purred. But Brady barely heard her as he raced Rafe toward the barn exit door.

A shout from Dan telling them to wait up, only made Brady move faster.

Damn! But his balls and cock were already stiff and sore with the anticipation of pleasuring JJ and he couldn't get to her soon enough.

JJ trembled as she heard the stomping of their boots coming up the outside stairs of the ranch, followed by the squeak of the mudroom door being opened. She'd managed to get C.J. down for her nap in the nursery and if they had any luck, the baby would sleep for a couple of hours allowing JJ some much needed play time.

She inhaled as she heard their voices quieten. Wasn't surprised in the least when they didn't come upstairs right away. She'd left them a little present right there on the bottom step. It was a big enough sized basket filled with condoms and some cute little adult toys she'd purchased online days ago and Blue had delivered via discreet packages yesterday with their mail.

Her heart began to thump as she envisioned how they must be feeling after so many weeks of no sex. Probably just as tense and excited as she was to finally get back into the swing of things. She'd dressed in black fish net stockings; a cute red see-through baby doll teddy and she wore the gold cowboy earrings they'd gotten her at Christmas.

She'd been surprised they hadn't remembered today was a special romantic day for couples. Not that the four of them were a traditional couple, but still, they had remembered the other years.

She didn't want any gifts from them. That's not what this day was about for her. They gave her gifts everyday by helping her with the baby and assisting her with her chores. To have a Happy Valentine's Day kiss from each of them instead of a friendly peck on the cheek when they'd gone out to work this morning, would have been nice though.

But she had caught on quickly, they'd forgotten today was Valentine's Day.

JJ frowned as she waited. Was she being selfish? They were so busy with the ranch, working outdoors all the time and coming home tired and then helping her. But lately they'd become a fever in her blood. A few times she'd even had the urge to just grab one of them and insist he make love to her right then and there. It had been torture waiting on those toys and this sexy negligee to be delivered and then waiting all day for the guys to come home. She'd already made supper and had refrigerated everything for later.

So much later.

"So, Dan, have you caught on what JJ meant?" Rafe chuckled as he watched Dan and Brady stare at the white wicker basket full of naughty stuff.

"It's been so freaking long, why in the heck would you expect me to catch on in a split second? At least I finally got it when she said tie me down," Dan shot back.

They fell silent for a moment as they studied the red cock rings, the red blindfold with little white hearts, the cute little heart-shaped handcuffs lying amongst the heart-shaped candy lollipops, and a life-like chocolate penis wrapped in plastic topped off with a big red puffy bow.

"I'm detecting a theme here, gentlemen," Rafe muttered. Guilt shot through Dan as he remembered this was supposed to be a special day. He'd blown it. Big time.

Hell, from their surprised expressions on their faces, Dan and Brady realized they'd blown it as well.

"I'm detecting we forgot something, gentlemen," Brady said.

"Man, talk about a guilt trip. With everything that's been going on, it looks like we forgot Valentine's Day, gentlemen," Dan said with a frown.

Man, JJ should be putting all three of them into the doghouse. Instead, she was giving *them* a gift despite them forgetting the importance of today.

"Man, this sucks. I hope she doesn't feel obligated?" Dan complained.

Brady shook his head. "I think this is the real deal. She's been more cheerful lately. More like her old self."

Rafe nodded in agreement. Come to think of it, Brady was right.

"Yeah, she's laughing more at my bad jokes. It was happening so slowly, I hadn't even realized it," Dan replied.

Man, JJ was the best in not getting ticked off because they'd forgotten. Suddenly Rafe didn't feel so bad anymore.

"Not to fear, gentlemen. The night is still young. I don't hear a baby crying and we've got one willing woman waiting for us upstairs. We've got a lot to make up to her for forgetting Valentine's Day. And I suggest we get our asses in gear and start by giving her the pleasure filled Happy Valentine's evening that she's looking for?" Rafe urged.

There was a round of eager nods as Dan and Brady both smiled.

"I do like your idea, Rafe," Brady replied with an eyebrow wiggle.

"And I'm thinking I'm in the mood to pleasure," Dan said as he gripped the handle of the basket.

Rafe seized Dan by his elbow, stopping him cold.

"Hold on. We can't just go rushing up there like bulls in heat. We'll scare her off. Settle down, my fellow bucks. Let's get our heads together and crack a plan."

JJ frowned as she lay on her bed and stared at the doorway. Still nothing. It had been at least fifteen minutes since the guys had come inside. There had been a volley of low murmurs and then she'd heard the shower running in the downstairs bathroom. Figured maybe they were cleaning up. She could wait. But not forever!

Then she thought she'd heard something in the hallway and when she'd gone to look, there had been no one there. Now there was nothing but silence.

What was going on?

Frustration gnawed through her. This was not what she had been expecting. She'd thought all three of them would come up the stairs, undress her, not that there was much to undress, tie her to her bed and start making love to her. Hard, fast, and rough, just the way she wanted it.

She frowned as she stared at her fishnet stockings and wiggled her toes. Maybe she should have invested in a pair of nice fancy high heels to compliment the outfit, just like she'd seen in the picture on the Internet? Nah, it would have been a waste of money and she hated heels.

A sudden noise in the doorway had JJ's head snapping from her feet to the foot of her bed. She gasped as she saw all three of her cowboys standing there inside the doorway.

They were clean shaven and dressed in the same fancy clothing that she had insisted they wear to the Christmas party weeks ago. Each man also had a bright red artificial rose pinned to their top. It appeared that her basket had clued them in that it was Valentine's Day.

She giggled. She recognized the roses. They had raided the fake bouquet she'd purchased at an inexpensive store and placed in a vase to brighten up her kitchen. Such handy men.

Best of all, they all wore their cowboy hats, giving glimpses of damp hair. It appeared they had all showered downstairs and in record time.

Ripples of excitement blew through her. Fully dressed men, weren't what she had expected, however, cowboy hats were always welcome in her bedroom.

"Wow," she whispered. "You guys sure do clean up nice. I've missed you and your hats."

"You look hot, JJ," Dan complimented.

"Hot enough to burn me up," Rafe growled.

"Sexy fever hot," Brady said.

He broke ranks with the guys and strolled around to the side of her bed.

"We snuck in to see the baby and she's out like a light," Brady said. He held out his hand to her and wiggled his fingers.

"Come on, baby. We want to show you something."

There was a mischievous gleam in his blue eyes and hesitantly she grabbed his hand and allowed him to help her off the bed. He grabbed the baby monitor from her night table, then pulled her past the guys and then into the hallway.

"Where are we going?" she asked Brady.

"Shhh, come downstairs. We don't want to wake the baby and we might if we stay up here."

Oh. She had planned on not crying out while they made love to her. Had thought she could handle the pleasure, but maybe she couldn't?

The guys remained silent as they walked her down the stairs. Brady pulled her into the living room and JJ smiled as she saw what they'd been up to.

As Brady set the baby monitor on a nearby bookshelf, she gazed around the room. They had taken out the short stemmed white emergency candles and placed them in cups on shelves along the living room windowsill and up on the fireplace mantel. The candles' tiny little flames flickered romantically, and a cheerful fire crackled and sparkled in the hearth, casting a sensual glow around the living room. The largest sofa had been laden with blankets and pillows.

"Very impressive. Are we having a sleep over?" she teased.

"A hell of a long one," Dan replied in a lust-filled voice that made her breath catch.

She noted the knotty-pine coffee table had been pushed out of the way, and the condoms from her basket had been arranged over the tabletop.

"Look up," Brady said in a husky voice as he held her hands tight.

When she did as he asked, she spied a mistletoe hanging above them and right beside it dangled the red heart-shaped handcuffs she'd put in the basket earlier. Rafe reached up and tugged the cuffs lower and she realized they were attached to a rope that was coiled around a ceiling beam.

She'd thought they would use the cuffs on her tonight up in her room, but these fellows obviously had something else in mind.

"Since we never got a chance to hang the mistletoe for Christmas, due to the baby arriving, we thought we would pick up with the mistletoe and carry on from there with the toys in your Valentine's basket," Dan said softly.

She trembled as Dan moved in behind her and to her left. Brady lifted her arms and a moment later he had her restrained in the handcuffs.

"We're really sorry we forgot today was Valentine's Day and we've missed you, baby. Missed this so much," Rafe whispered as he also moved closer behind her and to her right.

With every inhalation, their scents filled her lungs. Delicate soaps intermingled with each man's unique masculine smells of sexual need, dominance, and possession.

Brady turned to face her. His blue eyes blazed with heat.

"Sweetness, you're everything to us. The center of our world. We love you like crazy," he said softly.

Emotions welled inside JJ at Brady's intimate words.

"I love all of you too," she whispered back. Boy, did she ever love them.

"Hand me that chocolate dildo, man," Brady suddenly demanded. His gaze had darkened, and she heard the rustle of plastic as one of the guys removed the dildo from its wrapping.

"Here," Brady said softly as the life-like toy suddenly appeared in front of her face.

"I want to watch you lick it, so I can see how you are going to take me, later," he demanded as he touched the treat to her lips. She opened her mouth and licked at the cockhead. Sweetness sparkled over the tip of her tongue.

Who knew a chocolate cock could taste so good?

She opened her mouth wider and accepted the sugary shaft, feeling some of the melting chocolate dribble down her chin. While she sucked the treat, she imagined Brady as he thrust his cock slowly in and out of her mouth. Without warning, a luscious smooth chocolatey syrup flowed from the tip of the toy and entered her mouth. She eagerly swallowed, knowing the chocolate would give her much needed energy for this evening.

She heard their breaths quicken as she lapped and licked. Heard their soft moans and low curses as she sucked the chocolate cock deeper and deeper into her mouth.

Suddenly Brady swore and withdrew.

JJ jerked against her restraints and whimpered as Brady lowered his head and licked the chocolate from her chin. The toy was forgotten as he pressed his warm mouth to hers, delicately sipping at her bottom lip.

The hunger inside of her rose as Brady's tongue suddenly and boldly entered her mouth. Sparks rocked through her as his tongue touched hers. At first, he dabbed tenderly, tentatively exploring her length and then just like old lovers meeting again after a long time, his tongue stroked and caressed and made love to hers, sending a volley of shivers racing through her body right down her legs and into her toes.

Sensations rocked her as Brady moved his body slightly away from hers and impatient hands smoothed over her body. She could hear

Rafe's harsh breathing as he began to undress her. Could feel her breathing and impatience pound her as her fishnet stockings were removed. She stepped out of them. Then the rest of her clothing fell away, and Rafe's hot hands caressed her milk-laden breasts, tweaked her sensitive nipples, then smoothed along her sides and massaged her buttocks.

"She's wearing a plug," came Rafe's hoarse whisper.

If the plug didn't tip them off that she wanted more than oral from them, then she was going to have a frustration fit. Those thoughts disintegrated as animalist growls of approval erupted from Brady and flew right into her mouth. His kiss deepened, overloading her senses, bringing her into a wonderful lightheaded world of pleasure.

If those cuffs weren't holding her up, she swore she would have toppled right over.

Mercy! She had missed *this*. Missed the caring way their hands explored her curves. The primal sounds they made when they touched her.

As Brady kissed her and Rafe caressed her with possession, she heard the rustle of clothing as Dan undressed. Then Rafe's hands fell away, and she knew in the gentle yet seductive strokes on her flesh, that Dan had taken over, allowing Rafe to undress.

Suddenly Brady stopped the intoxicating kiss, allowing both of them to grab some much-needed air.

Their harsh breaths rippled through the room.

"Open your eyes, baby. I want to see the pleasure in them," Brady whispered.

She moaned at his sultry voice, and she had trouble opening her eyes. When she did, she gasped at how needy he looked. His cowboy hat had fallen off during the kiss, his cheeks were flushed, his lips were plump and red from the sensual kisses, and she keened softly at how his eyes sparkled dark with dominance.

"Are you sure about this?" he asked harshly.

JJ nodded jerkily.

"I want all three of you. Inside of me. I need your pleasure. Need you to make love to me," she hissed. She could hear the desperation in her voice and knew they could hear it too.

"We need you too, sweet thing," Dan murmured from behind Brady.

Suddenly Brady let go of her, stepped away and Dan was taking his place. He was naked, and her pussy clenched as she spied the cock ring at the base of his engorged cock.

"Oh, looks painful," she whispered.

"Painfully good," Dan chuckled. She loved the laugh wrinkles around his eyes, and the intent of dominance flashing across his face.

She shuddered as he teased her pussy lips with his cockhead and then she cried out her enjoyment as he massaged her ultra-sensitive clitoris.

"I love you, baby. Love you like crazy," Dan said. Sexual hunger made his voice sound strangled.

She could barely speak as Rafe's hands continued to travel over her buttocks with intoxicating caresses.

"I love you too, Dan." *More than you'll ever know*, she thought as she tugged against her restraints, wanting to wrap her arms around his neck. His forest-green eyes blazed with intensity and her heart just burst at having three men loving her so much that they would share her with each other with no jealousy. That they would tend to her baby with no complaints and make sure she was healthy and happy. She knew men like this just didn't grow on trees. Knew that she was luckier than her wildest dreams.

Dan lowered his head and she nipped gently at his upper lip, then lapped her tongue over the area making him groan softly. Then his hot mouth melted over hers in an impatient kiss that stoked carnal fires deep inside of her.

"I'll remove the plug, baby," Rafe said softly from behind her. JJ bucked as his calloused hands gently caressed her ass, to soothe her. But she was way beyond excited now and she moaned into Dan's mouth as Rafe tugged on the plug.

"Easy," Rafe whispered. He tugged harder. The plug stayed firm as her ass clenched around it.

It had taken several days to prepare herself for them. Agonizing days of feeling the fullness of a plug throbbing inside of her instead of a hot pleasure shaft thrusting into her from one of her cowboys. Now the time was here, and anticipation rocked her. It took all her self-control not to start gyrating her hips and simply fall into the pleasure they were swiftly creating.

"Your pussy is steaming wet," Dan moaned as he broke the heady kiss and sucked on her bottom lip.

His cockhead massaged her clit, the sensual touches bringing wonderous shivery sensations. She knew if she'd had access to her arms, she would have grabbed him and moved herself hard against him, sliding his shaft inside her. Then she would have been lost in a world of bliss. But they were more patient than she ever could be because Dan was slowly moving aside, to her right, and Brady was sidling in beside him.

Their dark looks intoxicated her. Mesmerized her. The softness of the fur-lined cuffs dug into her wrists as she jerked when both Brady and Dan lifted their hands. They cupped her heavy breasts, their fingers tweaking and tugging on her sensitive nipples, and then they lowered their heads. She moaned, instinctively knowing their intentions.

"Oh!" she cried out as their hot mouths enveloped her nipples. Since her milk had come in, she'd only had her baby at her breast, but now with two men there, suckling, everything had turned very erotic.

She watched in wide-eyed wonder as they pulled on her flesh with their mouths. Their sensual groans of appreciation as they drank milk from her, turned her on so much, she just about came on the spot. She'd been so mesmerized at the sensual pleasure their mouths were creating, she hadn't even felt the plug leave her body, until Rafe was kissing her ass cheeks. Literally.

She convulsed as his calloused palm cupped her clenching pussy.

"She's nice and wet," Rafe said in a thick voice.

JJ hoped that was the signal that they needed to start making love to her, but she shook those thoughts away. They still needed to prepare her, to lube her.

Oh, wow, how had she forgotten so much over such a short period of time without them? Her impatience was making her heady, thoughtless, and selfish. Yet their touches were making her crazy with desire.

The men continued to tease her. Hot mouths drew milk from her, and a sultry finger swept leisurely over her clit. How much longer would this exquisite torture go on?

She was breathing hard and trying to keen softly so she wouldn't wake the baby. But it was hard. So hard to keep quiet when all these wickedly delicious sensations were spiraling through her like tornadoes. Perspiration dotted her forehead. Her pussy and ass throbbed with need. Her breasts were erotically sore as the men continued to pull at her nipples and drink from her.

Her heart thundered in her chest at Rafe's next words.

"I'm going to lube you, JJ. Prepare you for us."

Yes. Hurry! Please!

But Rafe's warm palms continued to leisurely stroke and teasingly caress the curves of her cheeks, and she tensed as he moved his hands closer, toward the crack in her ass.

Have mercy. They're going to drive me nuts!

"Are you ready?" he asked.

JJ inhaled deeply and nodded erratically.

She couldn't stand this need as she envisioned how she must look. Standing naked in her living room. Her arms stretched high above her head, bound by handcuffs with two grown men sucking at her breasts, and another man teasing her butt with his sensual touches.

She was more than hot. She was on fire, and she was ready to be liberated from her sexual distress.

One of Rafe's hands slid off her bum and then she trembled at the slurp of lube. A second later, a lubed finger prodded against her sphincter.

"Okay, baby doll, breathe in deep," Rafe instructed.

She knew this. Knew what to do. She forced herself to relax and inhaled. She cried out as Rafe slid a finger inside and her anal muscles gripped him tight.

Rafe groaned sexily. Brady and Dan answered with erotic grunts. Their animalistic noises were music to her ears and heated blood thrummed through her at lightning speed. Rafe moved his finger softly inside her, pushing against tense muscles. He withdrew. More slurps of lube.

She moaned as he slipped two lubed fingers into her.

"Those sexy little noises are making me so hard, I cannot wait to take you," Rafe muttered as he lubed her.

The fullness of his fingers felt wonderful as he massaged in the lube. Seconds later, he slipped in three fingers. The pressure was exquisite. With mouths on her nipples and fingers deep inside her, she wanted to scream and find a way to her ultimate release.

Soon she was yanking on her restraints. Twisting between them, needing them, wanting them.

"Please," she finally managed to whisper.

Her plea appeared to be the magic word to break them out of their spell, because suddenly the men let go of her tender nipples. And the seductive hand between her thighs slipped away. The handcuffs came off and someone lowered her arms. Firm hands settled at her waist, steadying her.

Whispered endearments caressed her senses as they led her on shaky legs toward the sofa. Rafe was already lying down there. His engorged penis jerked and pulsed as he stroked himself and she stared at his immense size.

"Come on here, Jennifer Jane," Rafe urged. He still wore his cowboy hat along with a sexy grin.

It had been so long since they'd been intimate, that she'd forgotten Rafe's big size. Suddenly it seemed as if the hormone-induced fog that had embraced her since Christmas' birth had fully lifted, and she wanted nothing more than to mount Rafe, just as she'd always enjoyed in the past.

Dan and Brady helped her to climb over him, and she slapped her hands upon his broad chest as she came down on him. His brown eyes were so dark with desire they were almost black. He looked incredibly dangerous and dominating as he reached out to her.

His calloused hands curled over her shoulders, and he pulled her forward and down on him. She moaned as his big cock slipped into her quivering wet vagina.

"No mistletoe for me?" he complained, but she saw the amusement mingling with his lust for her. But she had no patience for his teasing. Fever lust raced through her and she *needed* the release she was craving.

"I'm on top of you. Consider me your mistletoe," she breathed against his mouth.

She squeezed her eyes shut and enjoyed the throbbing length of heated hardness buried deep inside of her. But she was desperate. Hot and impatient.

She took Rafe's mouth in a demanding kiss, sliding her lips over his with firm possession. His cock jerked inside of her, and he moaned as her pussy muscles clenched in welcome around his shaft.

She moaned as Dan's possessive hands slid onto her hips and she bucked and hissed as his cock pressed against her sphincter. She broke the kiss and gasped for air as Dan's shaft slid deep and fast into her anal canal. The pressure of having two strong pulsing shafts buried inside of her was bliss. The pleasure was sweet and the climax she craved was almost within reach.

Her thigh muscles tensed, and her inner muscles hugged Dan's invasion like a glove. But Dan managed to pull out quickly, ensuring no stimulation from Rafe's body onto her clit and she knew that stimulus was exactly what she needed now to climax.

Damn you, Dan!

"Open your mouth, baby," Brady urged.

She moaned and realized her impatience was making her selfish yet again. The guys needed their pleasure too! She sensed Brady's shaft was in front of her face. Knew he would be standing there right beside the sofa, awaiting his release as well.

She did as he asked. He filled her mouth quickly and she grinned around his shaft.

Another impatient one, just like myself.

He withdrew and slid into her again. In order to please him, she clenched her lips tightly around his rigid flesh. He bucked his hips and moaned, the sound was guttural and primal. He began a rapid and steady pistoning into her and JJ realized Brady didn't want or need foreplay. Neither did Dan as he slid in and out of her, his thrusts quick now and blissfully long.

Rafe somehow managed to squeeze his hands between their chests, and he began an erotic pinching of her sensitized nipples, while he whispered endearments into her ear. He bucked beneath her as Dan plunged into her again, this time Rafe's shaft frayed against her clit, encouraging her to writhe and gyrate.

JJ shivered as the three men pistoned and drove into her. They filled her beautifully and easily found a wicked rhythm that sent her flying right over the brink and into the release she craved.

Her mouth tightened on Brady's rigid flesh. Her body tensed. Her thoughts scattered. The red-hot orgasm spun through her like a storm and a killing pleasure swallowed her in one giant luscious wave.

She could hear them muttering the words *mine*, as she came. Could smell their musky scents of sex heavy in the air.

Dark sensations raced through her. Deep and dangerously addictive.

Oh yeah, she was back. All of her was finally back to normal and she loved it. Loved this.

She twisted between Dan and Rafe. Sucked harder on Brady. She moaned and hissed and keened her appreciation. Barely heard them as they cried out their own release.

Sensations and spasms devoured her. The exquisite pleasure left no part of her untouched. She sank deep. Became tangled within scorching oblivion.

During the evening, her men made love to her over and over, bringing the woman out of her so many times. JJ smiled as she spun into yet another pleasure vortex. She couldn't be any more happier than she was right now, and she knew deep inside of her soul that these three sexy men would always be her cowboys.

The End

More Cowboys Online
~ Jan Springer ~ Erotic Romance ~

Cowboys for Christmas
Cowboys Online 1 ~ Moose Ranch
Jennifer Jane (JJ) Watson has spent the past ten Christmases in a
maximum-security prison.
The last thing she expects is to get early parole, along with a job on a
remote Canadian cattle ranch serving Christmas holiday dinners to
three of the sexiest cowboys she's ever met!
Rafe, Brady and Dan thought they were getting a couple of male
ex-cons to help out around their secluded ranch, but instead they get
an attractive and very appealing female.

In the snowbound wilds of Northern Ontario, female companionship is rare.

It's a good thing the three men like to share...

They're dominating, sexy-as-sin and they fill JJ with the hottest ménage fantasies she's ever had. Suddenly she's craving cowboys for Christmas and wishing for something she knows she can never have...a happily ever after.

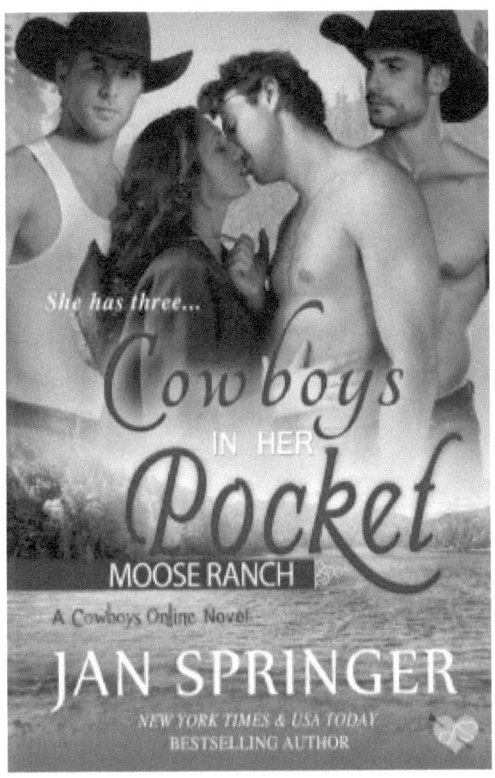

Cowboys In Her Pocket
Cowboys Online 2 ~ Moose Ranch

Jan Springer

After spending ten years in a maximum-security prison Jennifer Jane (JJ) Watson got early parole and a job on a remote Canadian cattle ranch playing housekeeper to three of the sexiest cowboys she's ever met...

Spring has finally arrived at Moose Ranch, and a single woman fresh out of prison shouldn't be experiencing scorching ménages with her three sexy-as-sin cowboys. But JJ's love for her men continues to grow as she gives into the fevered heat and scorching passions she feels for each of them.

Life is perfect.

Until her new life is tested when mysterious happenings occur on the ranch and then one of her cowboys is viciously attacked and injured.

Will JJ's newfound freedom and happiness be ripped away?

Rafe, Brady and Dan never expected to find an attractive and very appealing female to help them out at their secluded ranch. But in the wilds of Northern Ontario, female companionship is rare. It's a good thing the three men like to share...

Brady, Dan and Rafe have never been happier. Their cattle ranch is flourishing and their continued desire to share the sexy woman who cares for them makes their life complete. Until danger threatens to rip everything apart...

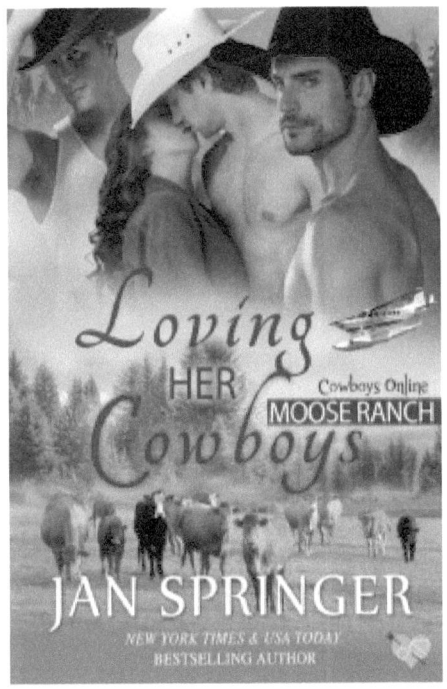

Loving Her Cowboys
Cowboys Online 3 ~ Moose Ranch
Jan Springer

AFTER SPENDING TEN years in a maximum-security prison Jennifer Jane (JJ) Watson got early parole and a job on a remote Canadian cattle ranch playing housekeeper to three of the sexiest cowboys she's ever met...

Her love for her cowboys continues to grow as she gives into fevered heat. But JJ's simmering restlessness explodes and she's seriously making up for lost time by pursuing her dreams. There's only one little problem. She hasn't revealed to her bosses what she's been up to while they're away tending to the cattle. She knows when they discover her secret, there will be hell to pay.

Ranchers Rafe, Dan and Brady have found the woman who completes them. She makes their secluded ranch a home-sweet-home.

She's vulnerable, sweet and willing to share her bed with all three of them. But when JJ's secret is unwittingly revealed, they're stunned and angry. They figure it's time to dole out some fiery punishment in some mighty naughty ways...

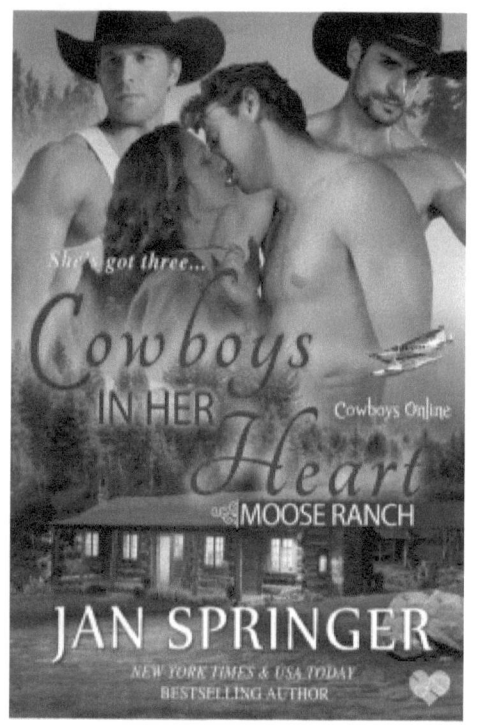

Cowboys In Her Heart
Cowboys Online 4 ~ Moose Ranch
Jan Springer

AFTER SPENDING TEN years in a maximum-security prison, JJ gets unexpected parole and a job on a Canadian ranch serving up scrumptious dinners and lots of hot love to three of the sexiest cowboys she's ever met.

Jennifer Jane "JJ" Watson has never been happier. She's going to have a baby!

Thankfully their wilderness ranch is a nice distraction for her three sexy cowboys while she's away flying her plane. But when she's home, her dominant hunks are tending to her naughty pregnant cravings and that includes plenty of sizzling ménages.

Rafe, Brady and Dan don't much like the idea of their woman flying the Canadian skies and being at the mercy of the unpredictable Northern Ontario weather. They would prefer having her warming their beds twenty-four seven. But she has a way of getting what she wants and right now she needs her new-found freedom.

Worst fears are realized when JJ, her friend and JJ's plane suddenly go missing and she doesn't come back home to them.

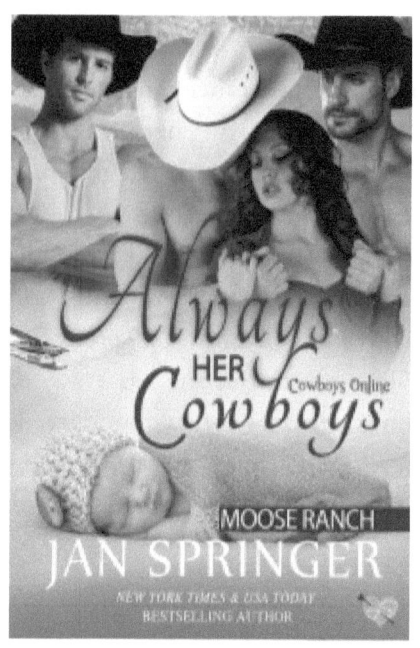

Always Her Cowboys
Cowboys Online #5 ~ Moose Ranch
A Canadian Contemporary Ménage Romance m/f/m/m

JENNIFER JANE (JJ) Watson has spent ten Christmases in a maximum-security prison. The last thing she expects is to get early parole, along with a job on a remote Canadian cattle ranch serving Christmas holiday dinners to three of the sexiest cowboys she's ever met!

Rafe, Brady and Dan thought they were getting male ex-cons to help out around their secluded ranch, but instead they get an attractive and very appealing female. In the snowbound wilds of Northern Ontario, female companionship is rare. It's a good thing the three men like to share...

Christmas is coming once again to Moose Ranch and with the due date of JJ's baby approaching fast, JJ is distracting herself from anxiety attacks by keeping herself ultra-busy preparing for the arrival of her baby and planning Moose Ranch's first annual Christmas party!

In having a wee baby on the way, there's a lot of stress for Brady, Rafe and Dan. Especially due to JJ's decision on having a wilderness mid-wife deliver the baby at the ranch house - *with* all *of them present for the birth*! But their concerns don't stop the men from showing JJ how much they love her...out of bed and in!

With wicked snowstorms, a grounded bush plane, a cheerful holiday party and a sweet little baby, the owners of Moose Ranch know this will be one sparkling Christmas season they won't soon forget...

Her Forever Cowboys
Cowboys Online 6 ~ Snowy Creek Ranch #1 (mfmm)
*AFTER SPENDING YEARS in prison, Milena Allen is conditionally
released and given a job at a secluded Canadian horse ranch where she's
instantly attracted to her three sexy cowboy bosses!*

When Cowboys Online sends Mitch, Daegen and Paul, a female
ex-con to help out around their wilderness ranch, they realize life has
been lonely without female companionship. Despite being without
women for so long, they vow Milena is off limits.

When violence threatens her cowboys, Milena's nursing skills are
put to the test, and she realizes she's falling head over straw hats for her
sexy bosses. Soon she discovers all three men are interested in her too!
But they keep treating her like one of the guys!

She's always wanted someone to love her and for a place that she
can call home. Can Mitch, Daegen and Paul, make her dreams come

true? Or will a horrific mistake by Cowboys Online unravel everything?

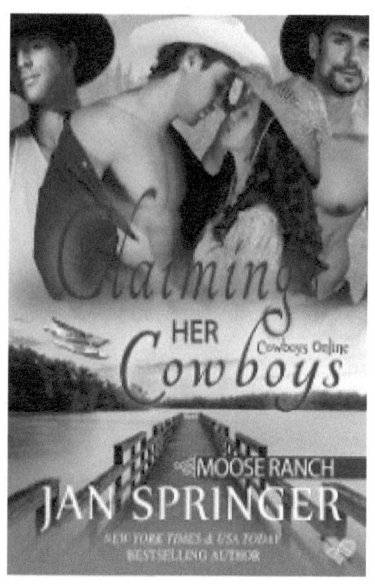

Claiming Her Cowboys
Cowboys Online # 7 Moose Ranch #6

Jennifer Jane (JJ) Watson spent ten years in a maximum-security prison. The last thing she expected was to get an early release, along with a job on a remote Canadian cattle ranch caring for three of the sexiest cowboys she's ever met!

Rafe, Brady and Dan thought they were getting a couple of male ex-cons to help out around their secluded ranch, but instead they get an attractive and very appealing female.
In the wilds of Northern Ontario, female companionship is rare so it's a good thing the three men like to share...

They're dominating, sexy-as-sin and they give JJ the hottest ménages plus one adorable baby!

But her second pregnancy comes as one giant surprise, and JJ's anxiety overwhelms her when she doesn't know who the father is.

Is it Rafe, Dan or Brady?

Spring days on this ranch are bursting with hard work, danger and emergencies but nights are filled with scorching passions and naughty pleasures as JJ lays claim to her three sexy cowboys.

Rescued by Her Cowboys
Moose Ranch#7 Cowboys Online#8
Jan Springer

Jennifer Jane (JJ) Watson has spent ten years in a maximum-security prison.
The last thing she expects is to get an early release, along with a job on a remote Canadian cattle ranch serving dinners to three of the sexiest cowboys she's ever met!

Rafe, Brady, and Dan thought they were getting a couple of male ex-cons to help out around their secluded ranch, but instead they get an attractive and very appealing female.

In the snowbound wilds of Northern Ontario, female companionship is rare.
It's a good thing the three men like to share...

When JJ embarks on a solo flight to the city for a fun-filled surprise wedding shower for a pilot friend, her trip is shattered when she's caught in a violent storm. She has no choice but to land upon one of the many desolate lakes in the unforgiving wilderness of Northern Ontario, Canada. After securing shelter on land, she teeters on the brink of despair when her float plane disappears on the lake of many bays.

Has her plane sunk? Or is it floating out there somewhere? JJ will have to tap into newfound courage in order to protect her unborn baby and survive while grappling with the uncertainty of rescue.

Rafe, Dan, and Brady are thrown into a desperate rescue mission when the woman they love doesn't come home. With the help of their pilot friends, they'll leave no stone unturned in their search. With little sleep and ongoing dangerous weather hindering their search, each cowboy must face their own fears about the possibility of life without JJ and the baby she is carrying.

Will they ever find out who the father of the baby is? Will JJ and her unborn baby make it out of the unforgiving wilderness? And can her three cowboys hold it together as they race against the elements to bring her home to her young daughter and back into their hearts once again?

Find out in Rescued by Her Cowboys.

Stories in the Cowboys Online Series:

Cowboys for Christmas ~ Book One – Moose Ranch #1 Cowboys Online #1 -Free

Cowboys in Her Pocket ~ Book Two – Moose Ranch #2 Cowboys Online #2

Loving Her Cowboys ~ Book Three – Moose Ranch #3 Cowboys Online #3

Cowboys In Her Heart ~ Book Four – Moose Ranch #4 Cowboys Online #4

Always Her Cowboys ~ Book Five – Moose Ranch #5 Cowboys Online #5

Her Forever Cowboys ~ Book Six – Snowy Creek Ranch #1 Cowboys Online #6

Claiming Her Cowboys ~ Book Seven – Moose Ranch #6 Cowboys Online #7

Rescued by Her Cowboys ~ Book Eight – Moose Ranch #7 Cowboys Online #8

Jan Springer Mini Catalog

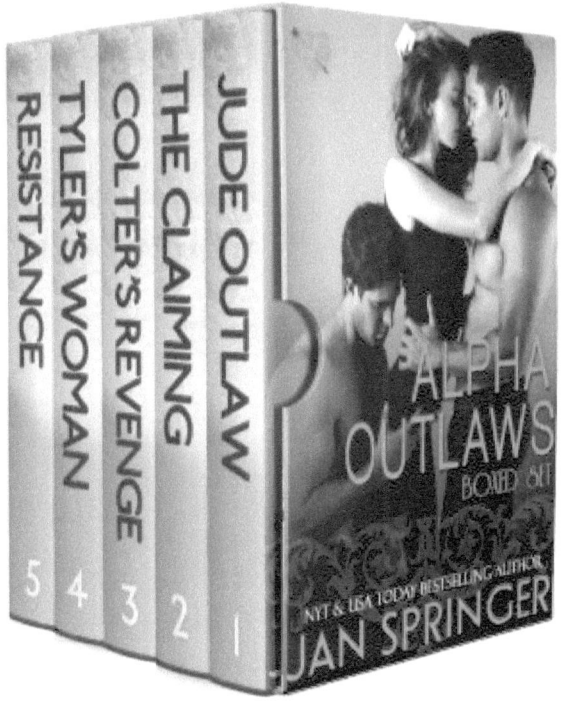

Alpha Outlaws Boxed Set
The Outlaw Lovers (Books 1 - 5)

A FAST-ACTING VIRUS has killed a majority of the world's female population. With so few women on Earth, a new law is created. The Claiming Law allow groups of men to stake a claim on a female—as their sensual property.

The Outlaw brothers have full intentions of declaring ownership of the women they love...and they'll do it any way they can.

This boxed set contains the first FIVE books in The Outlaw Lovers series.

Jude Outlaw, The Claiming, Colter's Revenge, Tyler's Woman, Resistance,

Some scenes include scorching ménages, romances, light bondage, bdsm, m/f/m/m, m/f, m/f/m, m/m, anal, oral, double penetration, figging, and more...

Please note: Tyler's Woman Book 4 in this series is not for sensitive readers.

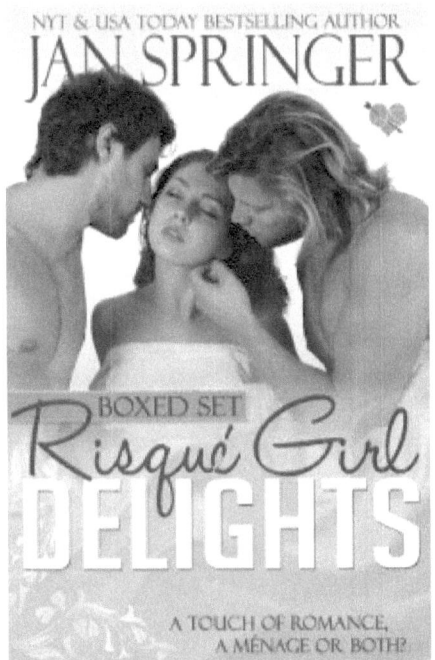

Risqué Girl Delights Box Set
A sizzling set of 4 contemporary erotic romances...Four women dare
to step out of the norm in the Risqué Girl Delights Boxed Set.
Includes sexy romances, naughty ménages, toys and hot alpha males.
Books: Edible Delights, Toygasm, Shy Girl, plus Roman & Julietta.
Edible Delights
YEARS AGO ALLIE MASTERS lost herself in the scorching passion
of a ménage a trois relationship with her two bosses. In order to regain
her independence, she walked away.

Max and Nick were very fulfilled with their gorgeous assistant.
The lovemaking was breathtaking and both men willingly shared the
woman they wanted to spend the rest of their lives with. Then she left.

Now Max and Nick have decided it's time to seduce Allie back into their lives.

Toygasm

IT'S A CASE OF MISTAKEN identity when the two owners of Sexy Toys, show up for an erotic several day photo shoot of their toys with famous nude model Cammie Creek.

Cammie believes the two hunks are the male models she's supposed to work with. Usually she doesn't mix business with pleasure, but when they're seducing her right there in front of the camera, she can't resist turning them into her own personal naughty toys.

Josh and Jode are enjoying the perks of being male models; hot lust, sizzling toys and the best pleasure they've ever had. But how will Cammie react when she discovers they're actually her bosses and not just male models?

Shy Girl

FINALLY FREE OF AN abusive relationship, "Shy Girl" Emma McCall sheds her inhibitions and explores her sensual side at Club Rendezvous, a club specializing in the Alternate Lifestyle.

At the club she's surprised to find Logan Masters, a sexy hunk she's secretly fantasized about since college. With Logan's help, Emma will experience her ultimate fantasy - a scorching ménage a trois.

Roman and Julietta

HER PERFECT LOVER...

Modern day pirate Julietta Black's life has always been immersed in the violent and traditional ways of piracy. When her family's arch enemy puts a hit out on her family, Julietta knows there's only one way to lift the hit; she must kidnap the enemy's sexy grandson and force a union between the two warring families. Night after night, wrapped in Roman's strong arms, she can't deny the searing attraction blazing between them. Nor can she deny he now holds her heart as well as her life in his hands.

His dream angel...

When Roman Prince's mysterious captor offers him a luscious woman to bed, fierce desire ignites, melting his usually tight self-control. Lust quickly turns to love as he enjoys their naughty trysts more than he should. How will he react when he discovers he's been kidnapped, not for a ransom, but captured for his sperm?

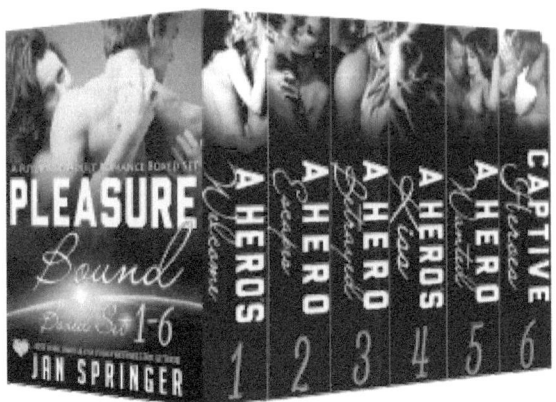

Futuristic Erotic Romance (m/f)
Pleasure Bound ~ The Complete Set ~ Books 1-6
A HERO'S WELCOME – Book One – Dr. Annie welcomes injured astronaut Joe Hero into her bed every chance she gets.

A Hero Escapes – Book Two – Queen Jacey's forbidden fantasies become reality and she can't get enough of well-hung Ben Hero's sizzling lovemaking.

A Hero Betrayed – Book Three – Fugitive-on-the-run Virgin must save Buck Hero who has been infected by a deadly virus. The cure? A twenty-four-hour making love marathon! But then she must betray him...

A Hero's Kiss – Book Four – US Astronaut Piper Hero is rescued by a dangerous stranger and can't seem to keep her hands off his luscious whip-scarred body.

A Hero Wanted – Book Five – A Hero is wanted for plus-sized Jenna who is finally able to explore her intimate side...where ménages are welcome.

Captive Heroes – Book Six – While searching for her brothers, Kayla Hero is bound and imprisoned by the Breeders— along with a male captive whose tantalizing scars pique her interest.

Injured and lost in a dense jungle, Kinley Hero is intimidated by the scarred man who hunts her, especially due to the power of erotic submission he holds over her.

Naughty Girl Desires Boxed Set
Contemporary Erotic Romance (m/f)
Includes: Jade's Fantasy, The Biker & The Bride,
Sinderella Sexy and Nice Girl Naughty.

Jade's Fantasy
In the land of the rich and famous, Kidnap Fantasies is the answer to
discreet naughty downtime.
When ex-downhill skier Jade Hart's two sisters give her a Kidnap
Fantasies questionnaire, Jade is aroused at the prospect of having
no-strings fun in the sun with a stranger whose only job would be to
fulfill her every intimate fantasy. Although she knows she's too shy to
send it in, she secretly pours her deepest wishes into the questionnaire.
Soon the questionnaire mysteriously vanishes and Jade's fantasy man
appears on her luxury yacht in the form of a sexy handy man who gives
her an intimate toy-filled Christmas holiday she'll never forget.

The Biker & The Bride
Wrapped in red-hot lust for revenge, Avery plots to murder the man
responsible for the death of her son.
Her plans are dashed when her ex-husband crashes her wedding and
whisks her away on his motorcycle to the rustic Canadian wilderness
cabin they'd once honeymooned.
Police detective, Mason is fighting for Avery's love with everything he
has.
Armed with whipped cream, handcuffs and his undying devotion,
Mason vows he will make Avery love again.

But it's only a matter of time before the man she'd planned to kill hunts them down...

Sinderella Sexy
By night, Dr. Ella Cinder, escapes reality by secretly performing in her own naughty version of Cinderella, aptly re-titled Sinderella. When sexy colleague Dr. Roarke Stephenson appears in the Sinderella audience on the same night her Prince Charming stands her up, Ella Cinder seizes the opportunity to make the man she's secretly fantasized about into her very own Prince Charming for one night of carnal fun in front of an audience.
But at the stroke of midnight, Ella knows she must face the harsh reality that Roarke can never learn her true identity.
Dr. Roarke Stephenson is immediately captured by the mysterious actress who hides her face behind a mask and is known only as Sinderella. For some insane reason, she reminds him of his klutzy co-worker, Ella. But that's not possible. Plain Ella would never have the nerve to do the wickedly delicious things Sinderella does to him, or would she?

Nice Girl Naughty
Blind since nineteen, Summer has blossomed into a famous wood carver.
When she's almost killed by a serial killer, she's whisked away to a secluded wilderness cabin by the man she once secretly loved. Summer can't get enough of touching professional bodyguard Nick Cassidy's thick, powerful muscles and all those other hard, yummy male body parts that she has always longed to explore.

For years Nick has stayed away from his best friend's kid sister, nice girl Summer. Now he's back, and sweeping his gorgeous redhead into the naughty cravings he's always had for her. With passion blinding him, Nick doesn't realize their hideout isn't safe—until it's too late.

YOU CAN GET A PEEK at more of Jan Springer's Erotic Romances at:

http://www.janspringer.com[1]

---

1.   http://www.janspringer.com/

Jan's Newsletter

Hi! If you would like to get an email when my books are released, you can sign up here:

English Newsletter: http://ymlp.com/xguembmugmgb

Your email addresses will never be shared and you can unsubscribe whenever you like.

Jasmine Black

Taken By Two Billionaires
Jasmine Black

Jill has always been warned that her gambling lifestyle would get her into trouble. And now *she's in trouble*.

She's lost a poker game to two very sexy billionaires, and they want *her* as their winnings.

They'll to do her whatever they wish...for an entire year.

On her way to her new life in Italy, while in a white stretch limo, Franco and Gianni will show Jill exactly what it means *to be won* by two billionaires.

Other stories in the Taken series
Taken by Two Prison Guards
Taken by Three Prison Guards
Taken by Two Sugar Daddies
Taken by Two X-Husbands
Taken by Two Personal Trainers
Taken by Two Firefighters
Taken by Two Bikers
Taken by Two Bosses
Taken by Two Cowboys
Taken by Two Doctors
Taken by Three Doctors
Taken by Three Bikers
Taken by Three Billionaires
Taken by Three Cowboys
Taken by Two Carpenters
Taken by Two Santas
Taken by Two Elves
More on the way

Jasmine Black Website ~ http://www.jasmine-black.com
Twitter ~ @blackerotica1
Jasmine Black Newsletter ~ http://ymlp.com/xghwwwmugmgj

About the Author

JAN SPRINGER WRITES full-time at her home nestled in cottage country, Ontario, Canada. She enjoys hiking, kayaking, gardening, reading, and writing. She is a member of the Romance Writers of America.

Ways to Connect

JAN SPRINGER WEBSITE at http://www.janspringer.com[1]
Instagram – http://www.instagram.com/janspringerauthor
Facebook - https://www.facebook.com/janspringereroticromance
Goodreads - https://www.goodreads.com/author/show/260628.Jan_Springer

Happy Reading,
Jan Springer

www.ingramcontent.com/pod-product-compliance
Lightning Source LLC
Chambersburg PA
CBHW020236030726
47497CB00009B/3126